The sarong remains embe¢
of people across South¢
related to clothing and fa
heritage, loved ones and
resonances with regard to
magically suffuses her narratives with all these sensations,
while confronting them with the paradoxes, imperfections
and the often uncomfortable realities of contemporary life.

PETER LEE
Co-author of *The Straits Chinese House* and
Honorary Curator, NUS Baba House, Singapore

Su Kim invites us into a powder room where gossip, sisterly
sharing and heartfelt confession remind us that nyonya
women living in a baba world had to have extra pluck to
transgress those social mores. In *Sarong Secrets*, she divulges
the nyonyas' colourful idiosyncrasies and guilty secrets with
ever so much wit and sympathy.

KHOO SALMA NASUTION
President, Penang Heritage Trust

Su Kim's stories may be short but they reveal the complexities
of the inter-cultural negotiations that constitute the identity
and reality of the Straits Chinese, a cultural hybrid whose
essence is mobility but whose existence is threatened by the
fast global changes that once gave it birth. The sentiments
that populate this book express acutely the exceptional spirit
of the babas and nyonyas and their silent struggle.

DR OOI KEE BENG
Deputy Director, Institute of
Southeast Asian Studies (ISEAS), Singapore

Reviews of Kebaya Tales

Like the generations of babas and nyonyas who traverse these stories, this book is a succulent mixture of colours, kebayas, *kerosang* and conversations, of scents, spicy food and feisty families. Su Kim brings her sharp eye, her love of stories, and her keen sense of the verbal and visual to this delightful book which gives us a chance to savour the richness and diversity of Peranakan lives.

PROFESSOR ALASTAIR PENNYCOOK
University of Technology, Sydney, Australia

Mothers tell stories. Daughters often forget them but not Su Kim. She shows that Malaysian Peranakan mothers transmit stories with a distinct flavour. Through these bright and trenchant vignettes, Su Kim has heightened the uniqueness of her community. One might add that these enjoyable tales also add a more nuanced dimension to the art of being both Malaysian and Chinese.

PROFESSOR WANG GUNGWU
National University of Singapore, Singapore

A fascinating collection of tales bringing together the uniqueness of traditional Peranakan culture with universal human themes. By turns deeply moving and deliciously funny, these stories and the lives they portray go on reverberating in the mind long after reading them.

PROFESSOR ALAN MALEY OBE
Leeds Metropolitan University, UK

Sarong Secrets

Of love, loss and longing

Lee Su Kim

Marshall Cavendish
Editions

Cover by Lynn Chin
Concept and layout of colour plates by Lee Su Kim. All sarongs, kebayas and
accessories featured are from the personal collection of the author unless stated
otherwise. Photography by Lee Jan Ming. Photographs belong to Lee Su Kim and
cannot be reproduced without the permission of the author.

Published by Marshall Cavendish Editions
An imprint of Marshall Cavendish International
1 New Industrial Road, Singapore 536196

Other Marshall Cavendish Offices:
Marshall Cavendish Corporation. 99 White Plains Road, Tarrytown NY 10591-9001,
USA • Marshall Cavendish International (Thailand) Co Ltd. 253 Asoke, 12th Flr,
Sukhumvit 21 Road, Klongtoey Nua, Wattana, Bangkok 10110, Thailand • Marshall
Cavendish (Malaysia) Sdn Bhd, Times Subang, Lot 46, Subang Hi-Tech Industrial Park,
Batu Tiga, 40000 Shah Alam, Selangor Darul Ehsan, Malaysia.

Marshall Cavendish is a trademark of Times Publishing Limited

National Library Board Singapore Cataloguing in Publication Data
Lee, Su Kim.
Sarong secrets / Lee Su Kim – Singapore : Marshall Cavendish Editions, 2013.
pages cm
ISBN : 978-981-4484-17-6 (paperback)

1. Peranakan (Asian people) – Fiction. II. Title.

PZ7
M823 — dc23   OCN859819664

Printed in Singapore by Times Printers Pte Ltd

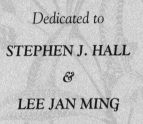

Dedicated to

STEPHEN J. HALL

&

LEE JAN MING

with love

*and to the memory of
my father, Lee Koon Liang
and mother, Foo Kwee Hoon*

Contents

Preface   9

Acknowledgements   11

About the Babas and Nyonyas   13

About the Sarong   17

Scarlet Revenge   21

Innocence   31

An English Afternoon Tea   49

Five Cents Bigger than Bullock Cart Wheel   61

Heaven Has Eyes   73

Frangipani   91

The House of Smells and Noises   103

Freedom in a Cage   119

The Tenant   139

The Collector   153

Lost in the USA   171

No More Roses   189

About the Author   203

Preface

I grew up in a world of sarongs. Grandma wore colourful, crisp sarongs, starched till they could function as mini changing rooms when left to stand on their own. My mother had a wider range — the *sarong kebaya* or *cheongsam* for formal functions and celebrations, cotton blouses with sarong or pants for informal wear. Grandfather was always in cool, checked sarongs whenever in relaxation mode. Father preferred pants and comfortable Pagoda T-shirts. Nightwear was of course comfy old sarongs for the adults.

The sarongs belonging to the women in my family were exquisite, made of fine *batik tulis*, in brilliant hues with amazing flora and fauna designs. I did not realise I was surrounded by living art moving and rustling all around me then. When Grandma passed away in the 1970s, and Mother in 1990, we nonchalantly placed their sarongs into their coffins, as precious possessions to accompany them in their afterlife. It was only much later I realised these sarongs were irreplaceable textile pieces of art, made by batik artisans whose quality of workmanship and skills are rare today.

I did not appreciate the sarong till much later, preferring the freedom of 'western' attire. Today like my grandma and mother, I wear them often, for formal events and informally. Whenever I travel, a sarong comes along with me in the suitcase. With practice, I have learnt to wear it properly and walk gracefully in a sarong. Just as the delicate nyonya kebaya inspired my earlier book *Kebaya Tales: Of Matriarchs, Maidens, Mistresses and Matchmakers*, this book is inspired by the sarongs and the fascinating community of babas and nyonyas who wear them.

Lee Su Kim
November 2013

Acknowledgements

I would like to thank Stephen Hall, who encouraged me at every step of the way. Thank you for your love and support — from ensuring that I am left in peace to write, sharing ideas, reading every draft as the story unfolded, helping with the photographs and captions, to revisions and editing. I am deeply grateful to you for without your gentle nudging, this book would not have been completed. To Jan Ming, thank you for all the beautiful photos you took for *Sarong Secrets* and for your interest in my book.

A big thank you goes to my friends, Harriet Wong, Lisa Keary, Gail Patrick, Neil Khor and Leslie Lim for their enthusiasm for my work and for urging me to continue writing. My thanks go to my artist friend Lillian Foo for the use of her lovely painting in my book. To Peter Wee, thank you for sharing your wonderful insights on sarongs and your kind hospitality always. To my sister Su Win, my brother Yu Ban, Philip Leong, Chong Mee Ying, my aunt Foo Kwee Sim, my uncles Foo Yat Kee and Yat Chin, cousins, nieces and nephews, thanks for your support.

I would like to acknowledge the kind assistance of Baba Lee Yuen Thein, Malacca, who enthusiastically dived into his grandmother's cupboards and pulled out vintage sarongs to be photographed when I sought help for more sarongs with motifs of food ingredients and cooking utensils. My thanks go to his grandmother Bibik Lam Ah Moi who kindly shared for this book project. To Don Harper, owner of the East Indies Museum, thank you for sharing your vast knowledge on vintage batik sarongs. My thanks also go to Hartono Sumarsono, author of *Batik Pesisir: An Indonesian Heritage* for your kindness and allowing me to use the photographs of two sarongs from your amazing collection of Pesisiran batik sarongs. To Nyonyas Lily and Rocky, Thank you.

I would like to thank all my friends in the Peranakan Baba Nyonya Association of Kuala Lumpur and Selangor (PPBNKLS) and the Peranakan associations in Malaysia, Singapore, Thailand, Indonesia and Australia for their support and enthusiasm. A unique cultural heritage that is in danger of disappearing only serves to push me further to document the stories of our community with its multiculturalism, colourful personalities and fabulous material culture.

It was a pleasure working with my editor, Mindy Pang. My thanks also go to Violet Phoon, Lee Mei Lin and the team at Marshall Cavendish, Singapore.

To all of you who have encouraged me to write more stories in emails, personal communication and Facebook, a big thank you. There are many of you — friends, family members, babas and nyonyas — who dance to a shared tune. *Kamsia* to all. With *Kebaya Tales* and *Sarong Secrets*, a certain symmetry is achieved. Still, there are more stories to tell.

About the Babas and Nyonyas

Origins

The babas and nyonyas of Malaysia and Singapore are a unique ethnic group which originated 700 years ago when Chinese traders arrived in Malacca, the centre of the Malacca Sultanate. The traders sojourned in Malacca for around six months, waiting for the monsoons to change direction and take them home to Fujian, on China's southeastern coast. They did not bring their womenfolk along and many intermarried with the local women. It was from these crosscultural unions that the babas and nyonyas evolved. Intermarriage between the babas and the local women eventually ceased, and for hundreds of years past, the babas married exclusively amongst their own people, becoming an endogamous and elite group.

Another interesting theory as to the origins of the babas and nyonyas is the legend of the Chinese princess, Hang Li Po, sent to marry the Sultan of Malacca to boost diplomatic ties between Malacca and China. The *Malay Annals* describes vividly the arrival of the Chinese princess Hang Li Po in Malacca with an entourage of five hundred ladies and courtiers. The princess and her retinue settled down at a place called Bukit China. The Sultan of Malacca, Sultan Mansur Shah, ordered a well dug at the foot of Bukit China for his Chinese bride. Both the well, Perigi Hang Li Po, and Bukit China are still in existence in Malacca today.

The babas and nyonyas are also known as the Peranakan, the Straits Chinese and Straits-born Chinese. The word 'Peranakan' is derived from the Malay word '*anak*' which means 'child'. The term refers to local-born as well as the offspring of foreigner-native union. Baba is an honorific from northern India for 'man', nyonya is an honorific for 'woman' in Malay adopted from the Portuguese word for grandmother.

Culture

The Baba nyonya culture is a rare and beautiful blend of many cultures – Chinese and Malay, mixed with elements from Javanese, Sumatran, Thai, Burmese, Balinese, Indian, Portuguese, Dutch and English cultures. The influence of European elements was because Malacca was conquered by three colonial powers successively: the Portuguese in 1511, the Dutch in 1641 and the British in 1825.

The culture is very much localised in essence, and proudly Chinese in form. The babas kept to their patriarchal culture, with male offsprings bearing the family name, while the mother culture was maintained by the womenfolk. In Malacca and Singapore, the Peranakan spoke Baba Malay, a patois of the Malay language with many loan words from Hokkien and English. In Penang, Hokkien was spoken instead of Baba Malay. The customs were heavily Chinese in form, as the babas and nyonyas clung loyally to their Chinese identity. Filial piety was very important and ancestral worship was core to the culture.

The lifestyle of the nyonyas was a unique balance between Chinese and Malay world traditions. The traditional nyonya costume was the *baju panjang* which can be traced to Javanese origins. It consisted of a long, loose calf-length top with long sleeves worn over a batik sarong. The collar is Chinese and the dress is fastened by a set of *kerosang* (three brooches linked by a gold chain).

By the end of the 1920s, young nyonyas abandoned the austere *baju panjang* for the more attractive nyonya kebaya. The short kebaya was more flattering and shapely, with intricate embroidery at the neckline, sleeves and hem. Nyonyas preferred the Pekalongan batik sarongs from Java because of their vibrant colours and motifs of birds, flowers and animals.

Nyonya food is a wonderful combination of Malay and Chinese cuisine with Southeast Asian and European influences. Using a variety of ingredients and cooking methods, herbs and spices and occasionally, western influences such as Worcester sauce, the nyonyas concocted a unique cuisine — the original fusion food with predominantly hot, spicy and piquant flavours. Peranakan cuisine is labour intensive and considered an art. Condiments are important on the nyonya's dining table especially the ubiquitous *sambal belachan*. A nyonya's cooking ability could be assessed, in the olden days, from the rhythms of the way she pounded the *sambal belachan*.

The babas and nyonyas today

Today, the baba and nyonya community still survives with its strongholds in Malacca, Penang and Singapore. Many younger generations of Peranakan have moved to live and work in Kuala Lumpur. (There are also Peranakan communities in Kelantan and Terengganu on the east coast of Peninsular Malaysia; Phuket, Thailand; Indonesia; Myanmar; Laos and Vietnam.) With globalisation and further migration, the Peranakans have settled all over the world with large communities in Melbourne, Sydney, Perth and London.

Both the old historic Quarters of Georgetown and Malacca, where Peranakan enclaves are located with its unique architecture and lifestyles, were declared World Heritage Sites by UNESCO in 2009.

About the Sarong

The Sarong is a garment worn by both men and women in many parts of Southeast Asia, in particular Malaysia, Indonesia, Singapore and Brunei. The word sarong is derived from the Malay word *sarung* which means 'sheath' or 'covering'. It is the traditional garment of Java and the Malay Archipelago, worn at all levels of society from the fisherman to the royal courts. It is known by different names in other parts of Southeast Asia, such as *longyi* in Myanmar, *sampot* in Cambodia and *malong* in the Philippines.

Sarongs are also worn throughout much of South Asia, the Arabian Peninsula, the Horn of Africa, and the Pacific islands. In Kerala, India, the sarong is called the *mundu* and worn mainly for religious and ceremonial purposes. In Tamil Naidu it is called *sarem* or *lungi*, in Saudi Arabia, *izaars* and in Oman, *wizaars*. In East Africa, sarongs worn by men are referred to as *kangas*, those by women as *kikois*. In the Pacific islands, it is known as the *pareo* in Tahiti, *kikepa* in Hawaii, *laplap* in Papua New Guinea, and *lava lava* in Samoa and the Solomon Islands.

In Southeast Asia, an ancient resist-dyeing technique known as batik is used to produce distinctive colours and patterns on fabric. A typical batik sarong usually has two sections: the *badan* (the body) and the *kepala* (the head) usually in a different colour or variation of the same motifs.

Some batik sarongs only contain a *badan* section. The finished sarong is a rectangular piece of cloth, and is worn either sewn together to form a tubular-shaped sarong, or worn left open as in a *kain lepas*.

The Peranakan Chinese women or nyonyas wear their batik sarongs with the *kepala* in front, secured with a silver belt. The batik sarong is the perfect complement to the nyonya's delicate kebaya. This is accessorised with jewellery, beaded shoes or *kasut manek* and beaded purses or silver bags. Nyonyas till today favour batik sarongs from Pekalongan, on the north coast of Java with its striking colours — scarlet, orange, peach, turquoise, shocking pink, mint green, teal, mauve, bold purple, brassy browns, sea greens and blues, saffron yellow, with motifs of birds, butterflies, flowers, garlands and animals from land and sea.

Although batik making was already well established in Java in the eighteenth century, a community of Peranakan Chinese settlers in Pekalongan produced a distinctive type of batik in the late nineteenth century which was a break from the sombre and more formal Javanese colour schemes and motifs. New, brighter colours became possible with the introduction of synthetic dyes and a demand for motifs blending tropical images and colours in a unique fusion. Incorporating Indo-European styles and free from strict symbolism, Pekalongan batik appealed to the nyonyas' love of colour and flamboyance.

Babas on the other hand, usually wore sarongs in light colours, or patterned in checks, stripes or plaid. They wore sarongs at home, never in a formal setting. Instead, their love of colour was manifested in Peranakan crockery and chinaware which they specially commissioned pottery makers to make in kilns in China and sent over to the Malay Peninsula.

Sarongs are highly versatile. Apart from its use as a garment, a sarong can be used as: head dress, scarf, shawl, blanket, table covering, wall hanging, fabric for making clothes, bed cover, beach wear, pillow, picnic mat and baby carrier. If caught in a situation where you need to change into your swimming gear or to get out of one, the sarong can act as an instant changing room.

My grandmother would change from her casual clothes of cotton blouse and sarong into her more formal, starched sarong and kebaya, without moving an inch from where she stood, all by using a sarong. Gripping her 'changing room' with her teeth with the sarong wrapped around her body loosely, she skillfully used both hands to tie her new sarong around her waist, then *berkemban*-style, slipped on her chemise and kebaya over her shoulders. The 'changing room' was then dropped onto the floor and picked up with a deft flick of her toes.

As a baby, I was rocked to sleep in a very comfortable cradle — a sarong.

Watercolour painting by Lillian Foo

Scarlet Revenge

It wasn't the right time to walk out yet. Walk out of her marriage once and for all. One day, maybe, but not now, not yet, she decided, staring at her reflection in the mirror. A woman in her mid-forties, a fading beauty with beautiful lash-fringed eyes and dark arched eyebrows, stared back at her.

'Liz Taylor eyes', he had whispered admiringly a long time ago when she was nineteen, fresh out of school. He used to pick her up after classes in his flashy metallic blue sports car and whisk her off to a nice lunch somewhere. How she blushed as he gallantly opened the door for her with a flourish and politely kissed her hand as she stepped into the automobile. Her girlfriends, some still suffering from acne, would swoon with envy and tease her tirelessly.

But now, that luscious bloom of youth seemed to have faded all too quickly. Her skin had grown pale and sallow, starved of sunshine, and two discernible frown lines insinuated upon her forehead. The hair around her temples whispered tinges of grey and delicate fine lines fanned harshly beside her eyes whenever she smiled — which was rarely.

They had three sons — the youngest just seven years of age. She had no choice but to wait for them to grow a little older. She did not have any income nor any skills to speak of. He had swept her off her feet when she was far too young and vulnerable. Her parents had urged her not to rush into any serious relationship at such a young age.

"Get a career first. Go to university, I'm willing to pay for your education for as far as you wish to go, Scarlet," her father advised.

"He's the first man you've met. He wants to start a family but you have your whole life ahead of you. Take your time, don't rush. Marriage is a lifetime," her mother too opposed the match.

He was twelve years her senior, the son of a company director, and very persistent. He was used to getting what he wanted. This charming young girl was, for the moment, on the top of his priority list. He was smitten by her fresh and dewy beauty, her sparkling laughter and innocent ways, and wanted her as his wife despite her parents' strong disapproval of the courtship.

One evening, while they were watching television at her home and her parents were out, he suddenly gathered her up in his arms, carried her to her bedroom and made love to her, even though she had tried to protest.

Soon she found out she was with child. The only recourse was to get married, with her parents pressurising 'the bastard' which was what her father called him, to marry her as soon as possible before she began to 'show'.

She peered closely into the mirror, and tried to smile. Her lips twitched into a semblance of a smile but her eyes remained lifeless, filled with repressed anger.

She was sick of him. Sick and tired of the abuse from her husband. Not the physical abuse — he never laid hands on her — but the verbal abuse was intolerable. The taunts on how ugly she was, a 'stupid boring housewife', an 'old hag'. The higher his status in society, the more successful his business, the more demeaning his comments. What was once passion had trickled into a vaguely remembered love, and now it had become a farce, two persons going through the motions of matrimony in appearance only.

Am I so disgusting? That ugly? She looked at her reflection, *Is there no hope?*

A sad aging beauty, with puffy circles beneath her eyes, looked back at her.

"Don't regret it, don't look back at your mistakes," her mother had told her before she passed away four years ago. *But how does one get out of a bad one?* Scarlet wondered. A few times, she had confided her problems to her mother. But her mother was not much help, her advice being the same stoic response, "You make your bed, you lie in it."

"Your dear hubby must be making big bucks," her chatty neighbour, Irene D'Cruz, whispered to Scarlet over the garden fence one day when her husband wasn't around, "Flashy car, high-tech gadgets, expensive suits, all branded stuff huh? And you, my dear Scarlet, slaving away at home like Cinderella who never gets to go to the ball. Why so unfair? How can you take it?"

"You have been a very good wife. I don't understand why he treats you so cruelly," Irene voiced her indignation to Scarlet when she dropped in another time to give Scarlet a slice of her freshly-baked carrot cake.

"Maybe I bore him. I'm not highly educated. He meets a lot of important interesting people, you know. I am just a housewife."

"Nonsense. Don't give me that 'just a housewife' excuse. That is not an excuse."

"I have neglected looking after myself. With three children, endless housework, I have become boring and ugly."

"There's no such thing as an ugly woman. Only an unloved woman," Irene fumed, "I don't mean to interfere, but you shouldn't just accept it, you know. Do something about it."

The unkindest cut was he started calling her 'a slut' even though she had done nothing to deserve it. He started to come home late from work, sometimes not appearing till the wee hours of the morning, reeking of smoke and whisky. Sometimes, he didn't even come home because of 'video conferencing calls at the office', he claimed. She wasn't even sure what the word 'slut' meant until she looked it up after another quarrel. She crept into his study, pulled out her dictionary from school days and read that she was a 'cheap, wanton woman'.

After another fight early one morning, she found herself on the verge of breaking.

"Can't you iron properly? My shirts are horrible! You have so much time while I work like a dog at the office. What do you do the whole day long? Stupid housewife. Slut, you cheap slut," he yelled.

"Stop calling me that name. What have I done to deserve this?" questioned Scarlet. The word drove her nuts, she hated being called that when she had given him everything, the best years of her life.

"Just a slut, that's what you are! Now get out of my way or I'll miss my plane," he growled before he stomped out to the chauffeured limousine waiting outside.

She locked the front door after him, went into the kitchen and wept. She reached out for the paring knife on the kitchen counter which she used to peel potatoes. She started to cut herself on her palms, tiny cuts she was sure no one could see. Her tears splashed onto the drops of blood on the stark white kitchen top. Startled, she hastily put the knife away, wiped away the blood and tears, worried her sons might wake up and walk into the kitchen.

She had to find a way to cope. She had no recourse to luxuries like marriage counsellors, nowhere to escape. He held all the purse strings. She had no skills to speak of after twenty years of marriage and total domesticity. All she had were her sons whom she loved dearly.

She decided to act when he had to fly to Dubai for a three-day trade convention. She told no one, not even Irene, her only friend. After he had left for the airport and her children had gone to school, she pulled out a few hundred dollars from her paltry savings hidden in a Tupperware container amongst the soya sauce bottles and containers of curry and cinnamon powder.

She stuffed the money into her grocery shopping purse and hurried out to the local beauty salon a short walk away. She paused outside the salon, then bracing her shoulders, gingerly stepped in. The shampoo girls stared at her dowdy appearance, her messy hair and pulled out a chair for her.

Scarlet browsed through a pile of magazines then pointed at the glamorous model pouting on the glossy cover of the latest *Vogue* magazine. The hairstylist nodded agreeably and coloured Scarlet's hair a flaming reddish-brown, restyled it into an exotic bob. After that, the manicurist painted her nails bright red, her first manicure and pedicure ever. It felt good to be pampered for once.

The next day, after the children had gone to school, she took out the last of her savings and headed to the shops again. The shop assistants kept suggesting clothes which looked too matronly. She ignored them and kept rummaging in the racks. Then she found it – the perfect dress – in scorching-red, figure hugging with thin shoulder straps and a plunging neckline. It reminded her of the divine red dress her namesake had worn in her favourite novel, *Gone with the Wind*. Scarlett O'Hara, her heroine, had stunned her enemies into a sullen silence as she sauntered into the room in a seductive dress. This dress looked a tad tacky compared to Scarlett's, but it would do. She bought the dress and headed straight home.

On the third day, she stayed home all day, prepared dinner, helped the children with their homework and tucked them into bed. Late at night, she changed into her scarlet dress, painted her face, dabbed on bright red lipstick, slipped on an old pair of stilettos and called a taxi to take her to a nightclub which she had read about in the newspapers.

The nightclub was called Flames, supposedly the hottest club in town. Its entrance shone of metal and chrome and seemed very unwelcome, coupled with the beefy bouncers watching every guest with hawkish glares. The music was jarringly loud. For a brief moment, she felt like turning back. She pulled the sequined straps of her dress down a little over her shoulders and walked into the room. It was dark inside with strobe lights piercing the room every few seconds. She groped her way to the bar, perched herself on a bar stool and tried to live up to her husband's favourite name for her.

It wasn't difficult — quite soon after, a stranger came over and started to chat with her. His strong after-shave was a put-off but she tried her best to be approachable. He bought her a drink, and another. The throbbing thumping music was enticing. She stepped out onto the dance floor and began to dance. She hadn't danced in years, the pulsating rhythms made her heart pound and her body gyrate and respond. The admiring looks all around her ... she assumed they were admiring ... she couldn't quite tell in the flashing, neon-lit darkness — but it made her feel attractive for once, even desirable. She didn't feel useless or stupid and maybe she wasn't that ugly, not really with all those men eyeing and hovering around her.

On the fourth day, her husband came home. The first thing her husband said was, "How's the share market? What's for dinner?"

Then he noticed her appearance. He stared at her, speechless for a minute. He said, "Wow!"

She paused and waited, daring to hope.

He continued, "Wow! What have you done to yourself?"

Her hand nervously reached out to her heart, and she waited for some more.

He exclaimed, "Now you really look like one. A real Slut."

She smiled. A twisted smile which grew wider and wider, a pained but satisfied smile.

The traditional costume of the nyonyas is the sarong kebaya. The nyonyas favoured batik sarongs from Pekalongan with their vibrant colours and complex motifs.

Pekalongan, a trading port on the north coast of Java, Indonesia, is renowned for its Pesisiran or 'coastal batik' style with its blend of Chinese, European, Arabic, Indian and Japanese influences.

Left: A sarong in scarlet

A parade of vintage sarongs belonging to collectors.

A batik sarong is a rectangular-shaped piece of cloth which has undergone either hand-drawn or block print motifs using wax-resist dyeing techniques.

Batik tulis or hand-drawn batik requires great skill and artistry. It is produced by artisans using a 'canting', a pen-like instrument through which molten wax is 'drawn' on the cloth. Batik cap sarongs are made by using copper printing blocks.

Right and Below: Artisans at a batik workshop in Solo, Java.

Innocence

Someone just touched my chest. A groping, creepy touch. I was only eight years old, a gangly little girl. It was crowded in Chinatown, bodies pushing and brushing against each other, in a last minute rush to do their shopping before the Chinese New Year in a week's time. That touch felt like a sinister fondling. In my child's mind, I didn't know what it meant, but even then, at eight years old, I sensed that the insidious touch was no accident.

I clutched my father's hand tighter. Again, that hand appeared from behind me — a thin hand with knobbly knuckles and bluish bulging veins, disembodied, poking in from the press of the crowds. It brushed against the front left side of my chest. I tried to scream but was voiceless with terror. I tried to tell my father but didn't know what to say. I didn't have the words, nor comprehended what that gesture meant. Instinctively, I knew it wasn't normal, people didn't go around touching little girls' bodies.

I turned around. All sorts of people crowded the five-foot-way. I noticed a thin, reedy man, in his forties or fifties, a short distance away, smiling at me. He was in a cotton singlet, collar bones protruding from a low-slung neckline, and faded baggy shorts. He had a sallow complexion and yellowing teeth. He looked down at me and gave a menacing smile, enjoying my helplessness and the fear in my eyes. I tugged at my father's arm, "Papa, let's go home."

"Huh? Don't you want us to get the fireworks? I know they sell it here somewhere. Ahh, I see it — there! Just across the road," my Pa said happily.

We crossed the road. I remember feeling a sense of relief, I was going over to the other side. I'd be safe there, on the other side, away from that evil prying hand. I looked behind me and clung again in desperation to my father as I saw the thin pale man crossing the road right behind us.

The crowds were even thicker on the opposite side of Jalan Sultan. People were busy bargaining and buying all kinds of stuff for the Lunar New Year — waxed ducks, Chinese sausages, mushrooms, dried longans, lychees, pots of blossoming limes and red lanterns amidst the aromas of chestnuts roasting in spitting hot woks, barbecued pork sizzling on the grill and the smoky flavours of toasted tofu and dried cuttlefish. The din of the vendors hawking their wares, the noise of the crowds, the loud music of Chinese springtime folk songs created a frightening cacophony. I clung to my father terrified I'd lose him and be sucked away into a dark incomprehensible world.

I kept turning around and saw the man following us from a short distance, the creepy smile lurking on his face, grinning perversely every time I turned around to look.

Papa finally reached the stall selling the fireworks.

"Here we are, Junie, let's choose some then we'll go home, okay?"

A pile of paper bags with thin red wooden sticks poking out caught my eye.

"Oh look Papa, Sparklers! Can we get some sparklers too?"

"Sure. Choose as many packets as you like. This time, we'll play to your heart's content."

"Papa loves playing with fireworks under the pretext of letting the children enjoy them," my mother would tease. My Papa loved me like crazy, I knew. I could have asked for the moon and he'd buy that for me if he could. If only I knew how to tell him about that hand, my father would have done something. But the groping hand was so bizarre to me, I still couldn't find the words to describe it to my father. Perhaps a sense of shame silenced the struggling voice within me too.

For a few moments, I forgot the menace and helped Papa choose all kinds of fireworks: fireworks that burst into laughing silver sparkles or golden showers, rockets that self-destructed with a loud bang or whizzed around like crazy ferris wheels, and of course, my favourite — sparklers! My brothers and I loved to play with them — watching them light up like joyous incandescent stars, twirling them around to form patterns for a few transient moments. I contemplated on how many packets of sparklers to pick up.

Then, again that offensive hand, pushing though the bodies surrounding the stall, fondling and squeezing my chest.

I burst into tears, "Papa, I want to go home. There's this ... this hand. There's a man, Papa ... following us."

"What? Who? Where?" Papa was shocked, looking around wildly, putting his arm protectively around me.

I turned around to point at the predator but he had disappeared. My eyes searched the crowds for the sallow, skinny man but he had gone, lurking, I'm sure, not too far away.

"He's gone! He was here a minute ago."

"Are you sure? Are you sure it's not just the crowds? Tell me what happened."

"Nothing, Papa. I just want to go home."

He lifted me up in his arms and carried me all the way to his car parked a distance away and drove home quietly. Once I reached home, I forgot all about it and was excitedly showing my little brother all the fireworks.

Nothing more was said of the incident.

The open courtyard at the back of the house, called the *tim chae*, was the most colourful place in my home. The sarongs that hung on long bamboo poles to dry lit up the place like a glorious art gallery in a swathe of colours. All the adults in my family wore sarongs. Grandpa wore white cotton sarongs while Papa loved slipping into his striped and checked sarongs to lounge around after work.

It was the women's sarongs, however, that took one's breath away. In myriad hues of peach, indigo, red, turquoise, teal, green and crimson, they were embellished with exquisite designs of flora and fauna. The sarongs came from

Pekalongan in northern Java where the Indonesian artisans created batik flights of fantasy that matched the nyonyas' love of colour and flamboyance perfectly.

My *amah*, Ah Chou, did the laundry in the early morning. After the sarongs were rinsed several times, Ah Chou would wring out the last few drops of water then string the tubular sarongs onto long bamboo poles. Each pole could take about four sarongs. Using a stick with a hook, she'd hoist the poles high up to straddle beams up in the ceiling, and there the sarongs hung, flaunting themselves in all their glory, drying in the brilliant sunshine.

While I remember those gorgeous sarongs, I do not have any memory of Grandma's undergarments. Come to think of it, I don't remember her ever owning a pair of knickers. The nyonyas of the past did not wear bras either. Their casual wear comprised simple cotton blouses with two large pockets covering the breasts. Otherwise, it was the beautiful and delicate kebaya, worn at special functions or at home if one had servants to do the menial work. Underneath the diaphanous, see-through kebayas, the nyonyas wore chemises trimmed with lace or embroidery.

The nyonyas' garments were daring and seductive, in contrast to their attitude towards sex. In my home at least, it looked like it didn't exist. For a long time, as we girls were growing up, the word 'sex' or anything related to it was never mentioned. But there must have been some steamy excitement going on, I'm sure, as Grandma had ten children and my parents had two daughters and two sons.

One day, when I reached twelve years of age, my mother and grandmother were waiting excitedly for me, talking in hushed tones in the front hall as I put my school bags away after walking home from school. They looked around to make sure no menfolk were within hearing distance. Mother broke the news to me in a secretive manner while Grandma stood by quietly with a peculiar Mona Lisa-like smile.

"Err ... Junie, I found your underwear in the laundry basket this morning with some blood stains on it."

"What? Blood stains? But ... but I didn't cut myself or anything."

"You probably didn't notice it. It's just the beginning. You have come of age."

"Come of age? What does that mean?"

"It means you are now a woman, no longer a little girl."

"Huh? How did that happen? What am I suffering from?"

"Oh no, nothing. Except now you must be very careful."

"Careful of what?"

"Careful with yourself and how you conduct yourself. Now this is what you must do." She pulled out a fluffy cotton blob from under her blouse and proceeded to teach me how to wear it.

"Yikes, have I got to wear this thing all my life?"

"Oh no don't be silly, just a while. It will soon go away."

"Aren't you going to take me to see the doctor?"

"No need. You will be fine. Now no more questions and go and take your lunch."

I went into the storeroom which doubled up as a changing room and put the 'thing' on as instructed. I saw some blood stains down there and felt utterly miserable. Great, this was just what I needed – some debilitating disease. I would bleed to death before I'd even fallen in love and no one seemed to care.

I waddled out of the room with the alien wad between my legs and called for my mother.

"Help, Ma. How am I supposed to walk with this thing between my thighs?"

"*Mak datuk, tak seronoh betul anak dara ni!*" exclaimed Grandma in horror, hitting her forehead with her palm in exasperation.

"Sssshhh ... stop yelling. You don't have to tell the whole world. Just get used to it, okay?" Ma reprimanded me sharply.

Again, that stiff embarrassment, that awkwardness when it came to things to do with one's private parts. It was obvious she didn't want any more discussion, she said she had to heat up my lunch and rushed off to the kitchen.

Meanwhile, Grandma sat down on the ebony *barleh*, fanning her sandalwood fan daintily and proudly declared, "Junie, listen, *dengeh betul betul*, now you are a woman, a real woman."

"I am? When did that happen?" I said totally perplexed. All I did was study some algebra, civics and geography at school that day and made yam cake and *agar-agar* jelly at domestic science class. How did that make me a woman?

"One day you will be a mother. You will bear children," Grandma continued, her eyes flitting, dancing from side to side, looking in the distant future.

"Ha ha ha, *Poh Poh*, so funny," I squealed with laughter, making Grandma a little annoyed but that didn't stop her from predicting the future.

"I can die happy. I know our line is assured. I know you are a girl but at least, there will be continuity. We won't die out, not yet," Grandma continued with her weird ramblings.

Then she lay down on the *barleh*, rested her head on the small stiff pillow and took her mandatory afternoon siesta.

After all that grand talk about offspring and progeny, strangely both my mother and Grandma didn't want to elaborate further. Both had dismissed the topic. I brooded the whole day, sulking that life had given me a horrible hemorrhaging illness. It was irritating how both women treated my affliction like a wonderful secret, smiling and nodding secretively at me, hugging something precious to themselves.

A week later, the bleeding stopped.

"I'm cured! My prayers have been answered," I disclosed triumphantly to my sister, two years older than me.

"Oh, for heaven's sake, it's not a disease!" retorted my grumpy sister.

"It's not? What is it then?"

"It's called the Period."

"Huh? What's that?"

"Every woman in the world has got it."

"Since when?"

"Monthly."

"What? How come no one ever told me? You mean ... you mean every ... every woman, every female? No way, that's not possible."

"Don't believe, done," grunted my taciturn sister, Julie, who never spoke more than five words at one time if she could help it.

I continued, "You mean even the Queen of England? Cleopatra? Marie Antoinette?"

"Yup."

"And Sister Agatha, our headmistress and ... and Cik Gu Ainon? And Miss Florence Fang, my hated Maths teacher? Ha, ha, serves her right! My word, how come I never knew this?"

"Well, now you know."

I spent the rest of the day in bewilderment trying to digest this incredible piece of information.

Apart from that, I had still not received any kind of sex education. Going to a very strict convent run by the nuns didn't help either. There was a chapter in our biology book called 'Fertilization'. On the day of that lesson, our science teacher, Sister Angus, a nun in a habit, didn't have a clue as well, using her ruler to point at the picture of the rabbit she had drawn on the blackboard, poking vigorously at its innards. Sister Angus warned us ominously in her lilting Scottish accent, "*Och*, you lassies must know rabbits breed like crazy. If *aye* were *ye*, I'd stay away from *dem* of the opposite sex."

The books I read did not give me any leads either. All the heroines in the Barbara Cartland novels I enjoyed were chaste English roses who were always rescued at just the right moment by some handsome, hunky Marquis or Viscount, and they all 'lived happily ever after', which didn't give a girl like me a clue as to what that meant. I noticed a book called *Lady Chatterley's Lover* in my father's library, but could never get my hands on it as Papa kept the glass door of the particular cupboard under lock and key.

Meanwhile, my body was changing shape. My hips became fuller and rounder, I was thrilled to wear a bra to school, graduating from the regiments of schoolgirls still wearing singlets under their school blouses. My world was still an innocent one, and my knowledge of the opposite sex and indeed, sex, in general was abysmal.

One day I was reading a book I found in my parents' library and was floored by a word I'd never come across. Too lazy to look for the dictionary, I decided to ask my father. His command of English was superb.

Papa was playing mahjong with three female neighbours when I barged into the hall.

"Papa, what's the meaning of this word 'rape'?"

A stunned silence. Pa was in the midst of pulling out a card from the deck of mahjong tiles neatly placed in a row when he froze at my question. At first, he kept quiet, reluctant to answer.

I waited impatiently. I wondered why all the ladies seemed to be waiting for Pa's answer. They had all stopped playing and were staring at Papa. Aunty Kongah started to examine the ceiling fastidiously, looking for geckos. Aunty Kay looked down under the table to check out her brightly painted toes, and Aunty Tong splayed her fingers out in front of her and began to scrutinise her multiple gold and diamond rings.

"Err ... ahem ... err ... hmmm ... where did you read that?" queried my father, frowning.

"I'm reading this book *Satan Never Sleeps* by Pearl S. Buck. There's this paragraph that says the girl woke up and found she had been raped. What's rape, Pa?"

He paused for what seemed like eternity then announced studiously, "It means a plant ... eh ... the leaf of the flax plant," Pa mumbled uncomfortably.

Aunty Kongah's head abruptly swiveled down to look at the floor, poker-faced, Aunty Kay ducked under the table making strange snorting noises, while Aunty Tong began to giggle and chortle, her chubby shoulders shaking with suppressed laughter, winking and blinking at her rings.

"Huh?" I said confused, "It doesn't make sense. A flax plant? What's flax?"

"It's a plant used to make linen," said Pa solemnly while the three ladies stared at him, mouths half-open.

Papa flinched as I persisted, "Linen? It says in the book, she wakes up and thinks it's rape. She finds that her blouse, her *samfoo* top has been torn."

Aunty Kongah tried to help, "Must be a linen *samfoo*!"

A loud yell ensued from her, "*Adoi, celaka*! Who kicked me-*har*? *Sakit, tau*? Very pain!" glaring at the other two ladies at the table.

"I don't get it, I just don't understand. Why is she so traumatised then?" I mumbled as I couldn't make head or tail of the story.

Auntie Kongah butted in again, "Must be *Satan-lah*! *Ooow, Celaka*! Stop kicking me-*har*, you two," she protested, giggling, curling up her short stubby legs and glaring at the two other ladies.

"It says here in the book she is in the room with this man the night before..."

"*Choy choy! Tai kat lai see*! Spare us the details, girl. How to play mahjong like this? Sure lose money-*oh*," groaned Aunty Tong in her heavily accented Cantonese English.

"But that's it, Aunty Tong, no details at all! She finds her clothes are torn, it's rape. She's been wearing flax. Corny or not?"

"*Aiyah*, why they all *ne'er* teach *anyting* in school *one-ah*? School *ne'er* tell you all this *ting* one-*meh*?" complained Aunty Tong.

Pa ended the discussion abruptly, "Junie, we're playing mahjong here. Please don't disturb us."

"Sorry, Papa," I said.

I walked away. I overheard Aunty Kay say something like my-my-the-things young-people-are-reading-nowadays.

Pa shot a parting question, "Where did you get that book?"

"From your bookshelf, Pa."

He harrumphed one more time, while the three ladies smiled and winked in some kind of conspiracy and waved me away, anxious to resume their mahjong game.

Now that was a long time ago. Today, I worry all the time about my daughters and my only granddaughter. My granddaughter is six years old — a curious child, who likes books and listening in on adults' conversations, perennially bombarding anyone who'd listen with questions. One weekend, she came over to stay with me as her parents had to go on a trip overseas. She had changed into her pink pyjamas with little teddy bear patterns, her hair brushed into two pony tails, her face buried in a book of fairy tales.

I looked at her tenderly and ached with anxiety. I had read unnerving cases in the papers recently about a schoolgirl gone missing while walking home, another gang rape and murder of two sisters in an oil palm plantation, and yet another abduction of a little girl walking out to the store to buy an ice cream.

I pulled her to me close and said softly, "Amanda, when strangers call you and offer you sweets, don't respond, run to somewhere safe, do you understand? There is evil out there, many bad people out to harm innocent people like you."

She looked at me calmly, the blacks of her beautiful eyes round and enormous, "Don't worry Grandma. I know. Mum and Dad have warned me about the dangers out there. I know if anyone tries to be funny with me, I must scream, 'Help, rape, molest'. I know about *pee ... pee ... da ... files.*"

"You mean paedophile? I'm glad your parents have given you a good education in these matters."

"Grandma, I even have a tracking machine. If I disappear, Dad has a GPS installed in my mobile phone, he will know where to find me."

"Oh? I need one too. Getting very forgetful nowadays."

"Nah, you're too old, Grandma. These guys aren't interested in you. It's young things like me they prey on."

"A long time ago when I was your age, a man did something to me. He molested me but I didn't even know then what was happening. I was just too ridiculously innocent," I shared with my granddaughter.

"You were my age? Really?" she crinkled up her nose and frowned, glancing askance at my wrinkled hands and thinning hair.

"Really. I was young too, you know ... once upon a time. I was absolutely flat-chested yet that sick, horrible man kept following and touching me."

My grandchild brushed away a wisp of hair that had fallen on her cheek.

"I'm sorry to hear that, Grandma, what the man did to you," she said, tears welling up in those huge, innocent eyes.

"Oh, don't worry about it. It happened such a long time ago," I reached out to give her a hug.

"If ever we find that man who did that to you, Grandma, we will castrate him!"

"Where do you learn these words? Do you know what it means?"

"Sure, I read it somewhere and Googled it — you cut off the genitals and throw them away. He will lose all his sexual desire and squeak like a girl."

"Okay, that's enough, darling. Quite enough," I said aghast at how worldy wise she sounded.

"Mum is forever warning me about sex maniacs and perverts all the time. Quite boring really. Boring. They're even in the house — in the computer. Full of perverts there too!" she chirped.

She clambered onto the sofa where I was sipping a cup of hot chamomile tea and curled onto my lap,

"Grandma, let's forget all this evil stuff, it's depressing. Can you read me something pleasant and innocent? How about a fairy tale? Can you read me the story of *Red Riding Hood?*"

Young nyonyas from the Peranakan Baba Nyonya Association of Kuala Lumpur and Selangor (PPBNKLS) and friends modelling vintage sarong kebayas at the National Textiles Museum, Kuala Lumpur. This event was in conjunction with the book launch of Lee Su Kim's book, Kebaya Tales: Of Matriarchs, Maidens, Mistresses and Matchmakers *on 8 January 2012.*

The brilliant colours of Pekalongan sarongs are loved by younger nyonyas, the perfect foil to the delicate kebayas. A typical sarong consists of the kepala *or head (right), and the* badan *or body (left).*

The tim chae *or courtyard in the author's family home, a prewar building at Jalan Sin Chew Kee, off Galloway Road, Kuala Lumpur. The photo shows a one-year-old Su Kim with her* amah, *Leong Yee.*

Lorong gelita tiada pelitanya
Terang bulan sinarkan cahaya
Sarong pusaka banyak ceritanya
Mama jadikan tanda mata

Sorong sampan ke tepi pelabuhan
Mudek ke hilir muatan diisi
Sarong lipatan tempat sembunyian
Baik dikilir sebelum dikasi

There's no street lamps in the dark alley
Only the moon shining forth her glory
Personal sarongs carry many a story
A perfect souvenir from dear granny

Pushing the boat next to the port
Sail to the estuary to load cargo
Neatly folded sarongs a perfect hiding spot
Better sieve through before letting them go

A *pantun* by baba Cedric Tan

An English Afternoon Tea

It would have been a perfect English afternoon tea on Joo Li's patio, surrounded by lush green plants, shady trees fringing a beautiful lawn, wind chimes ringing in the breeze and tinkling manmade waterfalls in a koi pool. As to be expected, my cousin Joo Li who prided herself on being a superb hostess, had prepared an exquisite spread — freshly baked scones, cucumber sandwiches, prawn cutlets and for that extra oomph, a pile of spicy-hot *sambal hae bee* sandwiches.

Her guests for her 'English tea', if there were such a thing, were her friend from London, Dr Lucinda Arthbuthnot, just arrived in Kuala Lumpur after a long flight from London, and I. The doctor was a professor of sociolinguistics from a top-ranking university, Joo Li proudly exclaimed when introducing Lucinda, renowned for her numerous publications on world Englishes, expecting me to coo sounds of approval. I, by the way, am Joo Li's rather insignificant first cousin, still struggling through my postgraduate programme in English Language studies at a local university. I suppose Joo Li figured I had something in common with the good professor as Joo Li's friends were mainly socialite types who lunched at trendy restaurants and frequented high-end spas and beauty salons.

After leading us out to her sunny patio, Joo Li called out shrilly in the direction of the kitchen, "Mila ... Mila, bring out the Earl Grey tea now," her voice a few octaves higher. The more excited she was, the higher her pitch, quite ghastly really.

No response. She trilled again, "Mila, Milagros, where is that Filipina maid of mine? MILA!"

"Yes, Marm?" came a low voice from the kitchen and out popped a brown face with short curly hair from behind the kitchen door.

"Ah there you are, Milagros. Bring out the tea," Joo Li commanded, "The Earl Grey, you hear? Not Chinese, not Japanese but the English, okay? Use my Royal Doulton red roses teapot, understand? And the silver tray!"

"Yes Marm," came the slow, sultry reply.

"And for heaven's sake, don't get it mixed up this time, English tea in English tea pot, Chinese tea in Chinese tea pot!"

"No, Marm."

"What an absolutely marvellous place you have here, Joo Li," chirped Lucinda looking around in delight, probably going through culture shock after flying in from dreary Heathrow.

"It is, isn't it?" said I, suddenly mindful of phrasing my question tags the proper standard English way.

"Oh *tee hee* ... no-*lah*. I mean, no, not really, it's just a small little place and so awfully messy," answered Joo Li, trying to appear modest, though we cousins all knew how hard she toiled to make her place appear like something out of *House and Gardens*.

"Might you want to sit down here, Lucinda, or how about over there in the wicker chair?" the hostess inquired of her English guest.

I rolled my eyes ... Heavens, Joo Li was beginning to talk as if she were the Duchess of Cambridge, enunciating her 't's and 'p's so spiffingly.

"Oh thank you, *darrl-link. Smashing,*" said Lucinda.

Just what I need, a *Downton Abbey* afternoon in this tropical humid weather, I mumbled to myself.

"And I, Joo Li dear, will seat myself here on this *dah-link* little marble stool by this cutesy fountain," said I facetiously.

"Oh, anywhere you like, Sim," replied Joo Li totally unconcerned where I planted myself.

"Lucinda dearie, do help yourself to some cucumber sandwiches," she chirped, passing her finest bone china platter of dainty sandwiches, cut in tiny triangles, to Lucinda.

"Cucumber sandwiches? Charming," purred Lucinda, "Did you make this?"

"Err ... well, yes and no. My maid made them, I taught her how to, and I did go out to buy the cucumber."

"Cucumber? Err, can I have the *sambal hae bee* ones instead?" I asked politely. 'No spice, not nice' was my life's mission statement.

It would have been a perfect afternoon tea, except for when Joey, Joo Li's eleven-year-old son, shouted *that word* right across the lounge from the huge leather sofa where he was hibernating. He didn't shout it actually, he spelt it.

"Mum, what's S-O-D-O-M-Y?"

"Whaa ...?" gasped Joo Li. Lucinda gulped, spilling Earl Grey all over her pleated skirt, while I got *sambal belachan* stuck in my throat.

"DON'T SHOUT, Joey. I'm not deaf. Why are you reading all that unsavoury stuff on the Internet? I told you to beware of pornography. Why can't you just read the newspapers?" scolded Joo Li.

"But Mum, I *am reading* the newspapers!"

"What? The newspapers? *Ala sial*!" yelled Joo Li.

"Oh, is that the name of the newspaper?" Lucinda asked curiously, "We have *The Sun* in England, quite titillating but nothing as spicy as yours."

"Oh no, Dr Abba ... err ... Arttbutt..." I began.

"Oh just call me Lucinda."

"Dr Lucinda, *Ala sial* is just Joo Li cursing. In a dying language — Baba Malay. We do that all the time over here," I quickly briefed her.

"You do?"

"Err ... no, not cursing but ... let me rephrase ... we lapse into our native tongues all the time over here," I clarified quite pleased with my ability to converse about the local linguistic landscape.

"Mum, it's all over the papers," shouted Joey, "Look Mum, a whole page on this *sod-doe-mee* trial. What is it?"

"Oh just ignore it, okay? It's full of crap nowadays," answered Joo Li.

I could see Lucinda wincing as she chewed the cucumber sandwiches nervously.

"Amazing. I thought this was a conservative, puritanical society," she muttered primly.

All I could say was the favourite trending slogan, "Err ... Malaysia *boleh*. Everything here *oso-can*."

Joo Li tried hard to deflect Joey, a top student in English Language, a lover of neologisms and crossword puzzles and stubborn as a pit bull dog.

"Joey, just forget it, okay? Read the Sports page like your father. Much better English there."

"But Mum," Joey persisted, "I *need* to know. I want to be a lawyer. Why do they want to put someone in jail for Sodo..."

"*Aiyyeee, gua takmau dengeh* ... I don't want you to say that word, you understand! *Hantu*, go and wash your mouth! *Celaka betul!*" Joo Li screamed.

"Dr Lucinda, don't you think my cousin Joo Li would be the perfect subject for my doctoral research? I'm collecting data on code-switching and swearing," I seized this opportunity to get free supervision.

Joo Li glared at me, "Not funny, Sim, not funny."

Joey yelled again, "Mum, more unfamiliar words ... what's 'rectum'?"

This time, all three of us spluttered on our tea.

"*Alamak! Betul sial budak ni. Shaddup!* There are ladies present here. You don't use such language in the presence of the fair sex, or any kind of sex. *Bodoh*, Stupid!" shouted Joo Li.

"But Mum, how will I know when I don't know the meaning of the word? *Du-uh*," Joey protested.

"Don't! Don't *duuh* me. I hate that word *Du-uh*. Mila," she screeched, "More tea please. We need a refill."

No maid appeared.

"MILA! Where's that maid of mine? Never around when you want her. Milagros Esmeralda Esperanza, more tea, please."

"Yes, Marm," I could hear Mila's low drawl from the kitchen.

Joo Li tried to steer us back to the earlier dulcet tones of the afternoon by talking of more important things.

"And so Lucinda, what's the weather like in England?"

"Oh, wet and soggy as usual."

Feeling sorry for my stressed-out cousin, I tried to steer the topic even further by posing the two compulsory questions that all Malaysians love to ask *Mat Salleh* visitors to this country.

"How long are you here for? Have you tried our durians?"

Before Lucinda could respond, it started all over again, this time with Joo Li's youngest daughter, six-year-old Tinkerbelle.

A cute child with freckles and hair in pigtails, she skipped into the room carrying her latest birthday present, an iPad.

"Here's my iPad. It can tell you anything. Everything!" she said, smiling excitedly while running towards her brother.

"Yay! Three cheers for Steve Jobs!" said Joey, stirring from the midst of the sofa, trying to pull himself out of the bundle of silk cushions he had amassed around himself.

"Oh no, don't touch it! Don't touch the iPad," Joo Li screeched.

Joey grabbed the iPad from Tinkerbelle and dashed behind the sofa with Joo Li chasing him, screaming, "Jonathan Tan Boon Keong, give that to me!"

Lucinda watched in open-mouthed fascination, holding her teacup poised in mid-air, her little pinky finger sticking out.

Just then, Tom, Joo Li's husband, walked in through the front door, "Hi everybody, I'm home. Joo Li, what on earth is wrong with you?" said Tom, shocked at the sight of his usually composed wife chasing their son round and round the sofa, screeching like a fish market vendor.

"Stop it, Joey. *Aiyeee* ... Give it to me. Right now, you hear me? *Celaka sial!*" Joo Li gasped as she huffed and puffed after her recalcitrant son.

"Stop what?" asked Tom, perplexed.

"Take it away from him, Tom! He wants to use the iPad to look up the word."

"Err ... Joo Li, isn't that a good idea? Wasn't that why we bought it?"

"Not if the word is 'sodomy'!" she screamed, "Our blinking newspapers has a sodomy trial splashed all over the front page and our dear son wants to learn a word a day. Told you to emigrate but you *dowan!* You and your *char kway teow! Cherkhek darah!*"

"WHAT? Sot ... sod ... what the ... hey, give me that iPad!" Tom joined the fray.

He lunged for it and was about to snatch it from Joey's hand when Joey deftly tossed it across to his sister Tinkerbelle, "Here, catch, Tinky."

Tinkerbelle squealed in delight, thrilled at this new game for usually the first thing her Dad did when he came home from the office was to look at his prize orchids.

Meanwhile, Dr Lucinda and I had been completely forgotten. Lucinda watched the goings-on fascinated while I, quite used to my dear cousin, the drama queen, tucked into more spicy sandwiches.

Tom managed to grab his daughter round her waist but Tinkerbelle, screaming and laughing, tossed the iPad back to Joey.

Joey caught the sleek black iPad in the rubber casing like a pro and began to search the forbidden word.

My toes curled up in apprehension, my *sambal* sandwich half eaten. Lucinda placed her tea cup down shakily and adjusted her gold-rimmed glasses tremulously on her sweaty nose.

As Joey typed the word on the screen, struggling somewhat with the spelling, everyone froze as if in slow motion, jaws dropping, eyes agog, antennae up.

Just then, Milagros stepped out from the kitchen with the refill, "Marm, tea."

In bounded Tom's huge Rottweiler, Bongo, wagging its tail furiously, saliva slathering the air. He could sense there's some kind of game going on and sniffed the air. He heads for Joey, smelled the iPad, instantly clamped his huge jaws on it and dashed out into the garden.

Everybody screamed and shouted in degrees of dismay.

"Oh no, come back, Bongo, it's not a toy, you stupid dog!" shouted Joey.

"*Waaah*, my birthday present! Got Bongo saliva," bawled Tinkerbelle.

"Hey Bongo, bring it back to Daddy, Bad Boy!" yelled Tom.

"Well, I never!" muttered Dr Lucinda Arthbuthnot.

I pronounced, "Ah, just another normal day in the life of a Malaysian family."

Only Joo Li seemed very pleased, "What a good dog, Bongo! I always knew he had potential."

Meanwhile, way down at the edge of the lovely green lawn, near the stands of exotic spider orchids, mighty Bongo spat the iPad out disgustedly with a loud 'grrroowwhhhh', probably finding the rubber cover highly unpalatable.

A Pekalongan sarong with swan motif by Lim Boen Hok, circa 1930s. These sarongs were influenced by the Dutch and Europeans, and are evocative of blue and white Ming china and Delft porcelain. (Courtesy of Hartono's Collection)

European influences are found in the culture and costume of the nyonyas, these include country garden themes, motifs of floral bouquets and animals such as swans and reindeers.

Left: A reindeer motif and garden motifs on beaded shoes (kasut manik).

Below: A beaded purse. (Courtesy of Harriet Wong)

English lace-trimmed kebaya renda *and* kebaya biku *in pastel colours. Garden motifs on kebaya sulam.*

Five Cents Bigger than Bullock Cart Wheel

"Dab some powder on your face at least, Bee Leng," I urged.

"No need, I'm already married. *Boh lang kwa.* Who wants to look at me?"

"It's got nothing to do with marital status. Your face is shiny with sweat," I said.

"Can't be bothered. Anyway, my hubby likes me the way I am."

"How'd you know?" I asked.

"He never complains," she replied with that annoying smirk.

"Well then, let's go," I said, feeling overdressed, all dolled up in lace and chiffon, a gold chain with a diamond pendant around my neck, compared to Bee, who wore a faded grey blouse and skirt. I had spent two hours at the hairdresser's, wanting to look my best for our old school chum, Lynette Lum's wedding dinner. We headed to the majestic E and O Hotel in the heart of Penang's heritage district, I wearing Chanel No 5 and Bee an ugly frown.

"I hope this is the last wedding dinner for this year. Fed up!" Bee grumbled.

"What? It's a privilege to be able to celebrate. I love weddings ... wish I could find a man," I sighed.

"I'm going broke giving out *angpows*. This is the third wedding banquet this year," she griped.

"Oh come on, don't be such a grouch. Let's enjoy ourselves," I cajoled, thinking to myself her *angpow* must be peanuts anyway. This was a woman who haggled for a discount with her dentist after a filling!

She was my best friend during secondary school days. We went our separate ways after school — she worked as a secretary in a construction firm while I went to university and graduated with a Masters in Business Administration from the US. After a decade living aboard, I returned to Penang to work in a multinational organisation. I had lost touch with many school friends and was delighted when I bumped into Bee Leng one day. It was like old times again — we'd go out for coffee or a meal whenever we could find some time. It was easier for Bee, as she had quit her job after her marriage, while I had a fulltime job and a demanding career.

But something had changed. She had become extremely tightfisted. During school days, it didn't really show as we didn't have any money. But now, I couldn't understand why the cheap clothes, the hand-me-downs from her sister which didn't fit, the visits to second-hand shops, the constant need to scrimp and save.

Her behaviour was worrying. She would pore over prices on restaurant menus, order the cheapest item, refusing to order drinks. At buffets, she would steal pastries from the buffet spread, stuffing them surreptitiously into her gigantic handbag. When grocery shopping, she would poke and prod the fish, the fruits, handpick shallot by shallot. Often, she walked with her head looking down in public places, "just in case someone's dropped a coin," she said.

A proverb in Penang Hokkien lampoons this sort of miserliness — *Gor chiam tua kuay gu chia lian*, which means 'Five cents bigger than bullock cart wheel'. Bullock cart wheels, in the past, were gargantuan. It was depressing that Bee had become such a scrooge.

One day, after we came home to Bee's place from a trip to the hypermarket, I tried to talk to her, "Bee, is there a problem?"

"Huh? What do you mean?" she queried, tongue sticking out in intense concentration, pouring water from a big bottle of mineral water bought at a bargain price into several small plastic ones.

"Are you having financial difficulties? If you are, I'd be most happy to help out, you must know that," I assured her.

"You are mistaken, my dear. My husband gives me tons of money. I am *drowning* in money actually," she said with a smirk.

"Then why are you so tight with it? Why so *kiam siap*? It's okay to spend a bit more, you know. You can't take it with you."

"Oh, you wouldn't understand. I came from a very poor family. I'm terrified it will all disappear. I get nightmares that one day all my money will be gone! I wake up in cold sweat sometimes, shivering I'm poor again."

"It's irrational, Bee. Why don't you seek professional help?"

"Don't be stupid. Shrinks cost money."

I was content to let things be, let her live with her phobia but I began to notice little signs that her miserliness was affecting her marriage.

Her husband Bryan was a successful business man who enjoyed the fine things in life. He appreciated good food, music, art and films, enjoyed socialising and travelling. Bee Leng loathed his expensive taste and called all his acquisitions 'baggage'.

"*Watfor? Watfor? Watfor* you buy this? Waste money only!' she'd scold Bryan whenever he came home with a box of chocolates or a bunch of flowers for her.

He was patient at first, always trying to cajole her into enjoying a bit more of life with him. But several times, I noticed a scowl, a flash of despair on his face.

One evening, I was having a drink with Bee at a coffee shop when her mobile phone rang. It was Bryan. She started screaming at him on the phone.

"Oh no, not another dinner again! Boring like hell. Standing for hours making small talk. You go by yourself. I'm not going, full stop!"

After a long tirade, she hung up on Bryan, tossed the mobile phone into her frumpy black bag and complained, "That stupid husband of mine ... wants me to go to another boring company function again! His boss' silver, gold anniversary, who cares? I refuse."

"Bee, just accompany him. Just bear it for a few hours, for his sake."

"*Watfor? Watfor? Watfor?* We don't have to cling to our husbands all the time, you know. But you wouldn't know as you don't have one. Anyway, I can't be bothered. Hate to dress up, talk rubbish."

"Your husband is rich and successful. Money is a great aphrodisiac, Bee. He's attending all these functions alone. Don't say I didn't warn you."

"Ha ha, so funny you are, worrying over nothing. I've gone through thick and thin with him. He is successful because of me, thanks to all my sacrifices. Solid and totally dependable, my Bryan. Besides, he's married — who wants him? Got grey hair already, no shame-*ah*."

I had known Bryan for a long time — we were all from the same school — he was my senior by two years, a school prefect and captain of the soccer team. I remember he was popular with the girls, quite a charmer with his boyish looks and athletic physique.

A few months later, from out of the blue, I got a call from Bryan from his office.

Hi Bryan, this is a surprise.

Can I ask a favour of you?

If it's not too impossible, sure, Bryan.

Please don't tell my wife I called you. Err ... can you please tell her to lighten up, if you know what I mean?

I know. I've tried many times. Stealing gold bars from Fort Knox is easier ... ha ha ... if there's any left, that is.

I can't carry on like this, counting every penny and sen...

I've tried, believe me, Bryan, many times.

I don't know what's wrong with her. She's a killjoy. It's driving me nuts!

I could hear his frustration. I jokingly teased.

It's all that money, Bryan. I think she'll be more normal if you didn't have all that money.

Looks like I'll just have to spend it all away, won't I?

Hey, don't give up on her. Keep on trying.

Well, thanks for listening. Bye.

Bye Bryan.

Over the next year or so, I spent less time with Bee as I had to travel quite a lot in my job. Truth was, her stinginess was affecting our friendship.

I didn't visit her anymore at her home in Island Glades. Not after I fell one evening on the steps of the split-level lounge of her house, groping my way through the dark. She had refused to switch on the lights as her electricity bill was far too high, she said. I didn't see the step, tripped and had to wear a cast for a month.

I was earning good money, I worked hard and wanted to enjoy myself. I hated her ridiculous parsimony. It all ended one day when she came to my place, bringing along a tea bag.

"Why, Bee? I have lots of tea in my house, you know that."

"Oh, it's like this — I'm doing this so that when you come to my house, *you* bring *your* own tea bag. You like drinking expensive tea so *you* buy *your* own expensive tea and bring it over to my place."

That's when I finally snapped.

I shouted, "Must you always count everything in monetary terms? Is that all that matters? How to go on like this?"

'Well, excuse me! I am going on just fine. It's you who's got a problem ... always going on about living life to the fullest, seize the day, blah blah ... like you're going to die tomorrow," Bee snapped back.

"Well, if I do die tomorrow, at least my eyes will be closed. Yours will definitely be wide open."

"Why, *see lang bin*, how unbecoming to talk like that! Like a ... like a frustrated old maid. You're jealous! Of my money, my properties, my husband. You poor thing, I'm leaving right now," she simpered, picked up her dumpy handbag and stomped out.

"Take your damn tea bag with you," I yelled.

We completely cooled off towards each other after that.

A year later, I was surprised to receive a call from Bee.

"I need to see you, I need to talk to someone," she said urgently.

"I'm not free. Got too much work," I dissembled.

"I need your help. For old times' sake, please."

We agreed to meet at the corner coffee shop near my office during my lunch break. I waited impatiently, sweating in the stifling heat amidst the noisy lunchtime crowd.

She arrived ten minutes late, sat down in front of me without a word. She removed her dark sunglasses, one side glued together with cellotape, revealing sunken red eyes. I was startled to see how haggard she'd become. She hadn't changed much apart from that, still dressed in a cheap polyester blouse, neckline fraying, a few threads hanging like stray cobwebs from the hemline of her skirt.

She blurted, "Bryan wants a divorce! He told me he's found someone else. Can you believe it?!"

I kept silent.

She babbled at breakneck speed, "That woman is half his age ... I hired a private investigator ... he's showering her with gifts, designer bags, expensive clothes, diamonds. He takes her out to swanky restaurants and trips abroad. First class ticket to London, Paris. *Loh mor liau*! Gone cuckoo!"

She pounded the formica-topped table with her fist, spilling the coffee. Heads turned in the crowded room but she didn't seem to care.

"He bought her a multi-million dollar apartment, a penthouse with a swimming pool, a brand new Mercedes. He *never* bought me anything! All our money is now going to this bloodsucker ... fooled by a money-grabbing, China doll, that stupid idiot!"

She lapsed into a string of expletives in Hokkien.

"He says she understands him, makes him feel like a man. I save all our hard-earned money and this is what he does to me! He never took me out for a nice dinner or a holiday, that bastard. Can you help me find a *bomoh*? Use black magic — make him come back to me."

My head spun. It did happen after all. 'Solid dependable Bryan' had cracked.

I read somewhere the most cruel thing to say to someone who is down and out is 'I told you so'.

I held my peace and said, "I don't believe in black magic, Bee."

"I don't care what you believe. I want him back! She can't have him! You've got to help me," she snapped.

I replied, "There's nothing I can do, Bee. I'm sure you'll find a way to get him back. I'm sure Bryan misses his wonderful life with you, that penny-pinching miser."

The wheels of progress keep turning even in the world of sarongs such as this batik kompeni from Cirebon, Indonesia. Batik kompeni is believed to have originated from Dutch batik makers and Ciribon batik artisans in the mid-nineteenth century. When humans were first portrayed in batik, they were usually imagined as employees of the Dutch East India Company.

Batik kompeni *is also known as* 'batik kartun'. *Note the whimsical designs and playfulness of the motifs.*

PENANG HOKKIEN IDIOMS

Chiak pa, Khoon
Tan jee oon
Khoon pa, Chiak
Tan ho giak

Eat till full, then sleep
Wait for opportunity
Sleep till full, then eat
Wait for prosperity

Keng lai, keng kee
Keng ka chau geng geng

Choose here, choose there
Choose till end up with lousy, bad choice

Heaven Has Eyes

Of all the relatives Peter enjoyed visiting during Chinese New Year, his favourite was still his grandaunt, Molek. She lived with her husband in a cosy, single storey bungalow with the curving bay windows and green terrazzo floor in the quiet town of Seremban, an hour's drive from Kuala Lumpur.

She would bring out all kinds of delicious goodies. He loved her homemade prawn crackers — crispy, crackling slivers flavoured with pepper, stored in huge Jacobs' cream cracker tins. She always served them with her homemade *Acar Awak*, a delicious concoction of pickled vegetables and pineapple in a peanut-laden spicy *rempah*. The peanut cookies, *kueh bangkit, kueh kapit,* fruit cake and pineapple tarts were all prepared by Molek. For Peter, the pièce de résistance was her *kaya*, a rich golden custard of egg and *santan*, steamed to a perfect consistency, served on dainty squares of *pulut tai tai*, glutinous rice coloured in bright-blue extracted from the blue pea flowers in her garden.

Molek was atypical of the feisty nyonya matriarch. Demure, shy and soft-spoken, she preferred to leave the conversation-making to her husband. Occasionally, she'd murmur gently, "*Makan, makan,*" urging her guests to eat to their hearts' content. She was always dressed in a simple *kebaya biku* and beautiful sarongs, her silver-grey hair neatly brushed up in a bun fastened with silver hairpins. Peter adored his gentle grandaunt who never had an unkind word for anyone.

Her husband, Chang, headmaster of the renowned Saint Augustine Boys' Secondary School, loved to talk politics and regale everyone with his impressive general knowledge and idiomatic expressions in his flawless English. Peter enjoyed listening to his granduncle's juicy gossip and stories. Molek would sit quietly beside him, smiling contentedly, opening up Milo tins to top up the crispy *kueh kapit* or deftly peeling mandarin oranges to fill the lacquer tray with more.

It was obvious the old couple loved each other, she attending to his every need, looking out for him in every way, and he, always trying to include her in his conversation, his eyes following her affectionately whenever she moved about the room. When Peter and his family left his grandaunt and granduncle's home the last time, Peter's mother sighed in the car on their journey home, "Now, that's a real love story. When two old folks in the twilight of their lives are still *in love* with each other, that's what I call *true* love."

Peter's father commented, "For as long as I've known Uncle Chang and Aunt Molek, they've never spent a day apart. They've been married fifty years or more, I think."

"Good Lord! Fifty years in love with the same person!" squeaked Emily from the back of the car.

"And you can't even stand your boyfriend after five minutes," Peter could not resist taking a playful jibe at his sister with her horde of admirers.

Five months later, that love story was interrupted tragically when Chang suddenly died of a heart attack after a fall in the bathroom.

After the funeral, Peter overheard his parents discussing Molek's situation.

"How is she going to manage, poor Molek? She will be lost without him," Peter's mother was troubled, "I've never seen two people so devoted to each other."

"She has two children, both successful professionals. I'm sure Teong and Carol will be there for their mother. They're both very good children," Peter's father assured his wife.

Peter was the first person to notice the taxi — the noisy crackle of its diesel engine rattling outside his house. He peeped out of the window and noticed a frail, old woman in the back seat groping desperately in her bag for coins. The taxi driver seemed to be scolding her, gesticulating wildly. The door opened and the elderly woman stepped out. The taxi sped away, its driver shouting at the top of his voice, "No money, don't take taxi-lah! *Chee sin!*"

She stood stunned for awhile, took a few faltering steps, and looked up and down at the row of houses. One hand clutching her handbag tightly to her chest, the other holding a tiny piece of crumpled paper, she swayed unsteadily on the hot tarmac. She peered at the paper, looking lost and bewildered. She was dressed in a mauve kebaya and dark green sarong, neatly pressed. Peter recognised her immediately and informed everyone, "It's grandaunt Molek! Look, Mother, Pa, Grandma, it's grandaunt Molek!"

"What? That's strange. She never steps out of her house on her own except with Uncle Chang when he was alive," Mother expressed her surprise.

They went out to greet her, feeling uneasy.

"It's good to see you again, Molek. Please do come in. Why are you all on your own? Why didn't your children bring you here?" Peter's grandma greets her cousin.

Molek shakes her head, distraught, unable to speak.

"Let's go into the house, it's cooler inside," Peter's mother says, certain something remiss has happened.

Molek stumbles on the uneven driveway. Peter, twelve years old, reaches for her hand and holds it protectively. She gives him a wan smile. Peter's father guides her in holding her by the elbow and places her carefully into the trusty old arm chair in the sitting room. Beads of perspiration roll down her forehead, her hands are icy cold. Peter's mother brings her a glass of warm water, his father switches on the ceiling fan. Grandma sits down beside Molek and asks her gently, "Are you alright?"

Molek sips a little water. She is trembling from something unspeakable, the fear hovers in her eyes. Peter is perplexed — this is unlike his grandaunt Molek Ee, always gracious, smelling of roses, vanilla and butter cake with her gentle ways and shy smiles.

"What is it, Molek? Is there something wrong?" Grandma asks again, fully aware this isn't a social visit.

Tears well up in Molek's eyes and in a soft voice quivering with shame, she says, "My son Beng Teong has disowned me. He and his wife chased me out of the house this morning."

The whole family is dumbfounded with disbelief.

A fluttering sound appears above their heads. Peter looks up and sees a large brown moth hovering near the ceiling flapping its wings loudly, unusual as it was noon.

I wonder if it is Grandpa? He did say he'd come back, Peter thought. *Or is it Granduncle Chang, who has come to listen to such heinous news?*

"What?" exclaims Peter's father, "But why? Your son Teong? But ... but ... I always thought he was a very good son."

"He was a good son all this while ... up till now ... or ... or maybe it was never quite sincere, I don't know. After Chang's funeral, they went to the lawyer's to find out the contents of Chang's will. I remember my son, Teong, and his wife walking into my home. I thought they were coming to spend some time with me."

She pauses to catch her breath, then continues, "But instead, Teong told me to pack up and get out, to leave my house immediately. My own house where I've lived all my married life."

"But it's your house, not his. He can't do that!"

"I think my husband made a terrible mistake. I am illiterate, not clever with legal matters and things like that. Chang thought it would be better that he wrote his will to put the house in my son's name, instead of in my name."

"Oh no," burst out Peter's parents.

Molek continued shakily, "Teong assured his father he would take care of me. I could continue to live in my home, just that the house would be in Teong's name to make everything easier. So my husband agreed. He trusted Teong. It never occurred to him we would be cheated by our own son."

"Your son is making good money. Why does he want your house? I cannot comprehend how a highly educated, well brought-up man from a good family can do something like this!" Peter's father is furious, shaking with rage.

"And Teong's wife — your daughter-in-law? Can't she stand up to Teong?" Mother asks.

"That Mimi, she's the evil, scheming one. She made Teong do this. My son would not have done this on his own. She pushed him to it. She said she didn't want to be stuck with an old person on her hands, that I was a burden on her lifestyle. She told me to go and live with my daughter instead."

"Ah yes, your daughter, Carol. The teacher, right? She would have some sense in her, better than your son, surely?

You can always go and stay with Carol," says Mother, trying to assure her.

Molek Ee's lips tremble, she can't speak, only her eyes reveal her horror.

They stare aghast at her, trying to read what her eyes are trying to say. It dawns on them that Molek's plight may be worse than they think for Molek's daughter's house is just a short distance away from hers. Yet she had travelled for more than an hour by taxi to their place.

Peter, puzzled, looks from one face to another. Mother has one hand clasped over her mouth, Father is frowning darkly. Grandma's lower lip quivers nervously, she reaches out and holds Molek Ee's shivering hands and asks, "Your daughter Carol? Don't tell me your daughter ... your daughter..."

Molek is weeping again, groping for her handkerchief tucked inside her kebaya. She sobs, "Mimi called a taxi and shoved me inside, screaming, 'Go, go to your daughter's. We don't want you here.' When the taxi arrives at my daughter's place, I see her, my Carol standing there at the door waiting. They must have called her to tell her I was on my way there. I thought she was waiting to receive me. I was safe ... I thought."

"What happened? One rotten apple is intolerable, surely not two?!" growls Father.

"Carol comes out to the gate but refuses to open it. Her arms are crossed across her chest, she has an ugly, bitter look. I've never seen her like that before..."

"What did she want?"

"She told me, 'Go back to Teong. *Balik! Balik!* Oh, Teong gets the house and I get the seventy-five-year-old mother, izzit? How unfair! Why didn't you and Pa give me the house, then maybe I'll consider taking you in. Even better — why not I get the house and Teong gets the mother!' "

Molek Ee sinks into the chair, drained, crying into her handkerchief.

"What a bitch," hisses Emily.

Molek shakes her head from side to side, moaning softly, "Useless, I'm a useless old woman. A burden to everyone. I should have died along with Chang. What have I got? Nothing. I have nothing ... all I have left are two monsters, my own children."

Tears roll down her cheeks as she relates further, "My son-in-law, Keong, and my grandchildren were standing at the door. I could see them, just behind Carol. They didn't say a word. Not a word. No one spoke up for me. I gave my children, my grandchildren everything. This is what I get in return..."

Peter sinks down on the floor beside his grandaunt, feeling helpless.

"We are not rich, just middle class folks. All we had was a house and some money to pass on to them, and yet, they can throw me out over that. I don't want to live anymore ... I want to join my husband..." she sobs.

Peter's mother puts an arm around her and tries to

comfort her, "Hush, don't talk like this, Molek Ee. Your children will come around, you'll see. I will pray for you."

Emily yelps, "Oh my God, to think I just submitted my project paper on Elizabethan literature!"

"What about it? And stop calling on the name of the Lord in vain, will you?" snaps Mother, irritated.

"Well, Mum, I argued in my VE 3053 paper that King Lear's rejection and abandonment by his daughters, Goneril and Regan, are a ludicrous stretch of Shakespeare's imagination, that this time he has truly taken his tragedies too far. And now, look at this — a real life case of children acting unnaturally, right under our very nose," elucidates the literary Emily.

"Here, stop changing the subject, will you all? This is really serious. I cannot believe that children, my very own relatives, can act this way. It's indecent, obscene!" Father fumes.

Grandma pulls out a huge handkerchief from underneath her starched cotton blouse, dabs her eyes vigorously and cries, "How can they do that to you? How can they? What ingratitude!"

Father tries to resolve the situation, "Don't worry, Molek Ee. We will take care of you. Stay here for as long as you like. I will call Teong and give him a piece of my mind. He has to take you back, he has to take care of you. It is his duty as a son. I will speak to your daughter too."

Molek Ee mutters, "*Kam sia lu, kamsia.* Thank you. I owe you all so much. Please forgive me for imposing on you like this."

Grandmother intones menacingly, "Don't worry, Molek. Heaven has eyes. You can be sure of that. As the Chinese proverb goes, *teen yow ngan* ... heaven has eyes."

Peter scratches his head.

"Really, Grandma? How will Heaven know? How many pairs of eyes has Heaven?" Peter asks quite baffled, as his mother is a Christian, his father an atheist, his sister a 'free thinker', and his Grandma practised a hodgepodge of everything. Grandpa, a staunch Buddhist, passed away a few years ago. On his death bed, he had told Peter not to grieve for him as he would be reborn again.

Peter searches for the beautiful moth. It is no longer hovering up in the ceiling. He finds it in a corner of the sitting room, flapping desperately, a jagged tear on the left wing. Tiny black ants are making their way towards it in a frenzied procession.

Peter asks aloud curiously, "Will Molek Ee's children go to Hell? Or will they come back to Earth as some lowly creature?"

"Come back as two lumps of shit, they will," comments Emily dryly.

"Here young lady, that's quite enough," Mother reprimands Emily crossly, "We sent you to university to get a good education, not become a Miss-Know-It-All!"

"I don't know what will happen, but as sure as hell, Heaven has eyes, Peter. I've lived long enough ... You'll see, Peter, one day, you'll see," Grandma says grimly, looking faraway into the distance, wiping her last tear with her fat, floppy handkerchief.

Molek Ee stayed with Peter's family for two months before Teong, her son, embarrassed by the many phone calls and admonishments he received from Peter's father, relented and decided to take his mother back home. One Sunday afternoon, Teong arrived with his wife, Mimi, to bring Molek Ee home.

Peter would never forget that scene. He was shocked by the way the old lady was handled, how Mimi scolded Molek Ee and behaved rudely to Peter's family, while her husband kept sullen, ashamed, head hanging low, refusing to talk to his relatives.

Mimi was in ugly form, screaming obscenities in Cantonese at her mother-in-law, shoving her once again into the car.

"Get inside the car. Hurry up, I don't have all day."

Molek crawled into the back of the car, acquiescent and frightened.

Mimi continued to harangue her, bending over and poking her head into the car, "Want to come back home, *izzit?* Come-*lah*, come and see how you like it. For Teong's sake, I've agreed to put up with you. We will take you back. But if you don't behave, I will *pok sei nei. Ngo pok sei nei keh tow hock!* Knock your head dead, I will!" scolded Mimi.

Peter could not take it anymore and angrily poked her in the bump, "Hey, don't talk to my grand aunt like that, you crazy woman!"

"Yeah, totally crass. Or are you really premeditating murder?" Emily butted in.

"Why, you two miserable twits, how dare you talk like this to me!" Mimi pulled herself out of the car and screeched, then turned on Peter's father.

"Don't talk to me about respect and honouring our elders when your own children are rude to me! No respect! Do you know who I am? I am Datin Mimi Tan..."

Peter's father retorted with utter disdain, "I don't care if you are a *datuk, tun* or *tan*. Yes, I know who you really are."

The last sight of Molek Ee was of her shivering in the back of Teong's car, pale with apprehension, her daughter-in-law in the front seat scowling, her mouth moving non-stop, while Teong drove off without a word of thanks.

Six months later, Molek Ee's face appeared in the Obituary in the newspapers in a small black and white photo. Peter's family was stunned; they had no idea she had been ill. Teong and Mimi, as well as Carol and her husband, had cut off all contact with Peter's family.

Peter and his family travelled to Seremban to attend her funeral. Peter's mother learnt from the neighbours that Molek had been treated badly, stashed away in a store room at the back of her house behind the servants' quarters. Even that was not good enough for Mimi and Teong. After a short period, they dumped her in a home for abandoned old folks.

An asthma attack knocked her out, they said, but Peter and his family knew better — she had died of a broken heart.

Peter's mother taught Peter and Emily to forgive and to forget. Peter found the forgiving part easy, it was the forgetting that was really hard. All his growing up years, he waited to see if his grandaunt would be vindicated. It didn't seem that way though for Teong and Mimi became more successful than ever, building up a business empire that eventually became a public-listed company. Their only son, a brilliant engineer designed a device using solar energy to power heavy machinery and made millions. As for Carol, they heard she opened a tuition centre after leaving the civil service, which became very successful in the small town of Seremban.

Years later, Peter, now in his early thirties, returns to Kuala Lumpur from Shanghai where he works to spend time with his parents during Chinese New Year. Grandma had passed away a few years ago. He is enjoying his breakfast in his parents' cheerful, sunny kitchen when his mother suddenly drops her cup of tea. It smashes on to the floor.

"What is it?" Father asks in concern.

"Oh my goodness, Teong and Mimi are divorcing each other in an acrimonious multi-million dollar divorce suit.

Both are accusing each other of cheating and stealing from the company funds. It's in the papers."

"What about their son? He's a partner in the company too, I think."

"Oh, didn't you know? Their son decided to give up everything sometime ago and has gone to join a monastery somewhere in Cambodia or Burma, I forget which. I read about it somewhere."

Peter and his father tries to absorb this news. Peter's mother is getting forgetful nowadays but they know she wouldn't invent something like this.

"And oh yes, I forgot to tell you this other piece of news. Remember Molek Ee's daughter Carol? Well, Carol's daughter, Teresa, called a few days ago to say they're putting Carol in a nursing home. Apparently, she eats non-stop and has become, in her daughter's words, 'disgustingly obese'. She cannot walk or move around anymore and has developed bedsores. They can't take care of her, they say, and have put her in an old folks' home."

Peter puts down his cup of coffee and lets out a long whistle, "Wow, looks like what goes around comes around."

A bright yellow butterfly flutters in from the garden and hovers above the kitchen table. Peter and his parents follow its flight, looking a bit surprised. It rests on the table awhile, then opening its wings to a lovely splash of yellow, it flutters around Peter's parents and finally settles on Peter's shoulder.

Peter is startled. He stares at the tiny butterfly on his shoulder. It sits there comfortably, tucking its wings gracefully together and blinks. Half-jokingly, he asks, "Err ... Mother, Pa ... *heh heh* ... do you think ... could this possibly be Grandma come to remind me of her Chinese proverb?"

"Oh Peter please. Let it go. That incident happened more than twenty years ago. Besides, Grandma is in peace in heaven, not flapping around as an insect," says Peter's mother.

"Yellow was her favourite colour though," teases his father.

The butterfly cocks its head, rubs its face with its front legs and winks.

Peter mumbles to the butterfly, "Okay, Okay, I get the message, Grandma. Heaven has eyes alright, and a powerful memory."

Butterflies are a much favoured motif in Pekalongan sarongs. Moths are rarely featured. Butterflies are a symbol of love and long life.

Above: *A contemporary* batik tulis *sarong by Hartono Sumarsono owned by the author (top) and a vintage sarong belonging to the author (below).*

Right: *A butterfly on a geometric banji (wanzi) or swastika background, a symbol of good luck. (Courtesy of Nyonya Lam Ah Moi.)*

Above: *The author's mother, Foo Kwee Hoon, carrying the one-month-old author, Su Kim, to the waiting car after receiving blessings at the temple. She is accompanied by the amah and her older daughter, Su Win, two years old.*

Above: *Whenever a huge moth entered our home in the day, paternal grandmother Chuan Neo, (in sarong kebaya) would consult her Chinese book on numbers before buying her lucky number from the local Chee Fah bookie.*

BABA IDIOMS AND EXPRESSIONS

Gedebak-gedebuk
Rough and heavy handed

Hiam
To criticise

Ho kua bo ho chiak
Deceptive (all that glitters is not gold)

Krepak-krepot
Gnarled and crinkled

Ho mia
To possess good fortune

Kam guan
Fully satisfied

Kek Khi
Annoyed or frustrated

Mulut pantat ayam
A blabbermouth

by William Gwee Thian Hock,
Mas Sepuloh: Baba Conversational Gems
(Singapore: Armour Publishing, 1993)

Frangipani

"Don't turn around, Mister," the passenger snarled. "Just give me all your money, then pull over."

Zaid did just that, handed the passenger his wages for the day, then pulled to the side of the road, with the six-inch knife hovering by his throat. The moment he stopped his taxi, the thug opened the door and ran away on foot, disappearing into the thick crowd outside the Golden Dragon Plaza. Zaid knew he did not stand a chance of getting his money back.

Kuala Lumpur had become a dangerous place, even for taxi drivers. This was the third time he'd been robbed. Two months ago, two teenagers with tattoos on their arms and metallic studs in their noses ran off without paying. Last year, a passenger had stuck a gun in his ribs and robbed him of his money, his mobile phone, even his last packet of cigarettes.

It began to drizzle. Whenever it rained, the roads in KL, especially during rush hours, clogged up like a massive heart attack. That's it, I'm going home. I've had enough, thought Zaid, police report can wait till tomorrow.

From a steady drizzle, it began to bucket down. Gusts of wind sprayed water against the windscreen, rivulets of rushing brownish water tumbled along the sides of the road. Within minutes the road was choked with traffic, drivers maniacally trying to squirm and bully their cars into every inch of space.

Zaid decided to take a detour along the old Sungai Besi road, a longer but less congested road to get home. The wipers were at full speed, yet visibility was down to just a few feet. He drove carefully along the narrow desolate road, straining to see ahead. He had not driven here for many years and was wary of the twisting curves and corners.

Suddenly, right in the middle of the road, a wisp of a girl emerged through the blinding whiteness. He cursed as he swerved wildly, missing her by a few inches.

She walked steadfastly to his taxi and got in.

"Crazy-ah? *Gila!* I almost ran into you!" Zaid exclaimed, shaken.

"Please, please take me home. I must get home," she answered.

"*Tak boleh.* Sorry, no more passengers. I want to go home myself," retorted Zaid. He had had enough for the day — robbery, lousy weather, traffic jams, suicidal characters.

He looked into the rear mirror, annoyed that she had clambered in without his acquiescence. When he saw how frail and pale she looked, his heart softened. Her clothes were drenched through, she was shivering from the cold.

"Please, please," she begged, "I must go home. They are waiting for me."

"Where is home, Miss?

"Waiting, they are waiting."

"Okay, okay, I'll take you home. Why are you here in the middle of nowhere? It's not safe, Miss. Where do you want to go?"

"I must go home. Take me to 4 Jalan Merbok, in Petaling Jaya, near the University Hospital."

Why, Zaid thought, she had the most beautiful voice, soft and husky, as if she were just whispering in his ear.

She brought a lovely fragrance into his taxi. The delicate scent of a familiar flower.

He couldn't remember the name but he was certain he'd encountered it somewhere. Through his rear mirror, he could see her trembling. Her long black hair was wet and plastered to her face and body. Her white dress clung to her slim figure.

"Miss, you are shivering. Here, take my coat. It will keep you warm." Zaid tossed his leather jacket over to her.

"Thank you," she whispered, her teeth chattering from the cold.

She put his coat around her shoulders.

He peeped at her through the mirror — he had never seen such a beautiful face in his life — sharp, delicate features in an oval-shaped face. She kept her eyes downcast most of the time but when she looked up, he was astounded to see a pair of almond-shaped, alluring eyes in an unusual light brown. She was very pale without a trace of make-up.

"How long have you been living in Petaling Jaya?" asked Zaid, trying to strike up a conversation with her.

"A long time."

She didn't seem keen to talk.

Zaid decided to leave her alone. He was content to steal a glance at her every now and then through the mirror. Her scent, perhaps it was her perfume, intoxicating and sweet, permeated the entire taxi.

Forty minutes later, they reached their destination. It was still bucketing down. She paid the fare and opened the door.

"Miss, wait, take my umbrella..."

Before he could finish his sentence, she had stepped out of the taxi, slammed the door shut and was swallowed up in the blinding, dazzling rain.

Zaid sighed. He would have liked to know her better. He wondered if he'd ever meet her again. He was surprised at himself – he had never felt this way towards his passengers. The scent of her, that beguiling, sweetish fragrance lingered a long while in his taxi and in his memory.

Two days later, Zaid found the perfect excuse. His coat! He remembered it was still around her shoulders when she got out of his taxi.

Ahh ... an excuse to see her again. Her fragile, distant beauty haunted him. He found himself thinking about her all the time.

He drove quickly to her house, he could still remember the way there. In the bright sunshine, he was surprised to see an old, dilapidated house; it needed a coat of paint badly. The windows were shrouded in thick dark curtains. Flowerpots containing dead plants lay strewn on the mangy, handkerchief-sized lawn. The porch was full of junk, an old bicycle lay on its side rusting and unused. Everything looked in a state of decay.

How could someone so beautiful live in a dump like this? he thought.

He pressed the doorbell. No one answered. He tried again and again. Finally, the door creaked open slowly. An elderly woman in a white blouse and a blue and white sarong appeared. Her silver hair was tied in a bun on the top of her head, untidy wisps of hair fluttering about her face.

"What do you want?" she asked in a weak quaver. She looked listless and tired, her shoulders hunched, carrying an invisible unbearable weight. Her eyes squinted in the sunshine, unaccustomed to the light.

"Good morning, Madam. Your daughter borrowed my coat two days ago. She forgot to return it. I have come to collect it."

"What daughter?" the old woman answered.

"The young lady who lives here. She was my passenger. I drive a taxi, you see. It was raining heavily and I lent her my coat. She told me this is her home..."

"How dare you? What kind of cruel joke is this?" she shrilled, her voice trembling in anger.

"What? I don't understand. I dropped her off, right here two days ago. I lent her my coat because she was cold."

"No one has come here for weeks, no one," she mumbled.

"But ... but she did come home. I dropped her off right here, in front of this house."

"She can't. She can't come home," she said, distraught.

"Why can't she come home?"

"She can't because she died. Forty days ago."

"But ... but I gave her a ride home."

Zaid stepped back in shock when the old woman howled in despair and screamed at him, "Go away. Go away. How long more must I suffer?"

"But my ... my coat?"

"Go away, there's no coat here," she shouted, slamming the door in his face.

He turned and left, shaken and in disbelief.

He jumped into his taxi and drove towards the old Sungei Besi road. Slowing down as he passed the spot where he had picked up the girl two nights ago, he noticed a cemetery beside the road.

He parked his car by the side of the road and got out. A hauntingly sweet smell filled the air. Zaid could feel his skin crawling as he realised the scent was the same fragrance of that cold rainy night. He followed the scent up a gentle incline to where a frangipani tree stood, shedding its lovely white flowers upon a solitary grave with a black marble tombstone.

The words on the tombstone revealed that a person named Anna was buried there, she had died just 40 days ago. Still skeptical, Zaid peered at the black and white photo on the tombstone. A lovely, young woman, with a heart-shaped face, long jet-black hair tumbling down her shoulders, stared back at him. Her eyes seemed to bore into him. He felt his blood turn into ice as he recognised her face. He stepped back in shock and stumbled over something lying on the floor. Resting peacefully on the floor was his brown coat, neatly folded.

He turned abruptly and ran, shouting in horror, tripping and falling, trampling on the lovely flowers, the scent of frangipani clinging to his clothes, his nose, almost smothering him.

Blue-white sarongs, known as batik kelengan, were worn by nyonyas in mourning in Malaysia and Indonesia. The mourning period lasted for three years in the past. Blue and whites were worn at the second stage of mourning, after black attire in the first stage.

Jewellery worn by the nyonyas during mourning were in silver, embellished with pearls that resembled teardrops.

Above: A set of silver kerosang earrings and pendant.

Right: A pearl and silver kerosang. Kerosangs used for mourning are called kerosang tuaha.

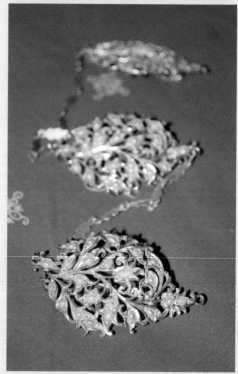

Above: *Blue and white kebayas.*

Left: *A sarong worn during mourning.*

Sulam kebaya ayam itik
Daun pokok sama ikan
Lukisan hidup sarong batik
Nyonya pakai menunjukan.
Ketam batu ada tangkap
Letak semua satu peti
Jangan simpan saya harap
Banyak rahsia dalam hati.

Chickens, ducks sewn on kebayas
Leaves as well as many fishes
Look so alive on sarong batik
The Nyonya wears for all to see.
Caught many hardy crabs
Kept them all in the big chest
Hope you're not keeping,
Many secrets in your heart.

A *pantun* by baba Chan Eng Thai

The House of Smells and Noises

Kai lived next door to a house with the most unusual smells and noises.

In the mornings, the unmistakable rhythmic tune of chilli and *sambal belachan* being pounded in a stone mortar, or the grinding of the *batu giling* as fresh red chili morphed into a glistening paste. The crack of crab shells being prised open, the metallic twang of a stainless steel cleaver smashing garlic pips on a wooden board, the chopping rhythms of shallots expertly sliced, the hiss of prawns in batter dipping into sizzling hot oil, the slap-slap of homemade fish paste tossed against the sides of a bowl.

If it wasn't the sounds, it was the smells that assailed your senses — a whiff of fried chicken marinated in turmeric, or a spicy dry smell that would make your eyes smart, sometimes the hint of a *babi pongteh* simmering in a cavernous claypot causing Kai's taste buds to tremble with anticipation.

It was the aroma of the curries that was the most mind-blowing ... the spicy-sour mouth-puckering scent of a prawn and pineapple curry simmering in thick tamarind juice or the rich *lemak* scent of a fish curry flavouring the air. Curry powder frying in a pan of hot oil perfumed with curry *pillai* leaves and cinnamon made Kai go weak in his knees. And the smell of *belachan* paste grilled over the fire was pure ecstasy.

The best kind of 'noise' was his neighbour Manis' voice as she called over the dividing wall at the backyard, "Kai, what are you doing today? Come over for lunch."

Manis loved to cook and was always inviting Kai over for a meal or snacks. This morning, she called out excitedly.

"Hey Kai, you free today? I'm cooking *ayam buah keluak* today."

"*Buah keluak* curry? Wow, Really?" The mention of it sent tingles of joy through him. Her *ayam buah keluak* curry was to-die-for.

"I managed to get really good *buah keluak*. Four kilos! My friend Halim hand-carried them all the way from Jakarta. The best from the market at Tangerang. I've soaked a basin full of the nuts for a week, they should be ready. Want to join us for lunch?"

In a heartbeat, Kai responded, "Yes, Aunty Manis! Will be there!"

The first time Kai tasted the *buah keluak* curry, Aunty Manis showed him that inside the crinkly, ugly black nuts lurked a blackish paste that tasted heavenly when cooked in a curry. "Don't judge a *keluak* by its cover, Kai, *ha ha ha*. Now taste it and tell me whether you like it," as she scooped out the insides of the nut with a teaspoon and dribbled it over Kai's steamed rice.

"It is absolutely ... I don't know how to describe it ... divine," drooled Kai, instantly smitten.

"I knew you'd love it. It's been called the truffle of Southeast Asia. Nothing quite like it, and no words in English to describe its taste," enthused Manis, her eyes twinkling happily.

The smell of the curry was wafting over now ... an incredible aroma of lemongrass, turmeric, chilli, *bunga kantan*, *buah keras*, tamarind ... He could visualise it bubbling away like lava in a cauldron, and Manis, on tip toes, peering into the enormous *belangah*, stirring the mixture lovingly as if it bore the secrets to eternal life.

"Roll out the Barrel ... We'll have a Barrel of Fun..."

He could hear her singing as she pottered about her kitchen. This was followed by 'It's a Long Way to Tipperary' with much gusto. Kai noticed amusedly her choice of songs — when the *rempahs* were sizzling away in the pan, she'd burst into lively numbers such as 'Jingling Nona', or 'When the Saints Go Marching In', when her curries were simmering, purring contentedly on the stove, she would croon old, sentimental numbers like 'Bengawan Solo' or 'Smoke Gets into your Eyes'. He found this ability of Manis to break into song spontaneously quite amazing. Kai could only whistle softly, he had never sung aloud in his life.

Kai's house smelt of rubber. Throughout the entire house, the suffocating smell of rubber assailed one's nose. His parents were suppliers of cheap rubber footwear to small retail businesses and night market vendors. In the front hall loomed a giant pile of slippers of all sizes with rubber straps in red, blue and green. In the dining room and kitchen, more boxes of cheap sneakers were piled high up to the ceiling, teetering or staunchly upright, waiting for their turn to shod mankind.

Kai hated the mess but had long given up trying to clear it. Often, suppliers or customers would drop in and out tumbled slippers and shoes, as they foraged through the pile, tossing the slippers carelessly back into the mountain of footwear if they were not the right size or colour. His parents didn't seem to mind the unnerving clutter and disarray. Maybe they never even noticed.

Kai's parents worked long hours and did not have time for their children. In his leisure time, Kai's father preferred to drink at the local coffee shop. Often he'd come home, drunk, spitting and cursing, tripping over the slippers that had fallen off the pile. His mother found her pleasure in gambling, retreating to an illegal gambling den a bus ride away to play mahjong every evening.

She never cooked for the family, resorting to hawker food instead. Sometimes there was nothing to eat when she went straight to gamble after work. Kai would go through the paltry supply of tinned food and cook something for his two younger brothers, unless Aunty Manis had cooked extra, which was often the case, and sent food over.

Kai enjoyed spending time at his neighbour's place. He was always welcome in Manis' home as she had a soft spot for the intelligent young man, with his courteous ways and curious mind. Although never articulated, both Manis and Kai recognised that he was the son she would have loved to call her own.

Dropping in to Manis' home was like slipping on the most comfortable old clothes. Her home was cosy, full of wood, rattan, plants and interesting curios. Kai loved hanging around, especially in the kitchen, where Manis was in her element. Just under five feet, chubby, with dimples in her cheeks whenever she laughed, she could multi-task like no other. She could whip up a sumptuous meal of five to six dishes, make pickles, *kueh* or jams, bake, then cook an entirely different meal for dinner all in a day.

Once, after she'd taken out a big bowl of coconut cream and a plate of fruits from the fridge, she dropped a ladle on the floor. Just as Kai reached out to help, she bent over slightly, slammed the door of the fridge shut with her butt, then with her right foot, picked up the ladle with her toes, put down the plate of fruits, flicked up the ladle deftly bending at the knee, and caught it expertly with her free hand, never once spilling the cream.

"Aunty Manis, I guess you never have to say 'Help, I've got my hands full'," he said laughingly in admiration.

"Ha ha, the *pantat* ... err ... I mean, the backside, is very useful for many things," she commented then roared with laughter when she saw Kai blushed.

"Don't mind me, Kai. I'm an old lady now. When I was young I sure knew how to turn it on, you know," she chuckled, dimples dancing on her cheeks.

Kai was curious about her name and asked her one day.

"Aunty Manis, how come you have such an unusual name? It's a Malay name, isn't it?"

"Oh, it's my father's nickname for me. My real name is Swee Neo. 'Manis' is a shortened version of '*hitam manis*'. My colouring is like *kopi susu*, coffee with milk, my Pa's favourite drink. When I was young, I got teased by my schoolfriends for being 'brown'. I came home from school one day, crying, pining to be fair like my lily-white friends.

Pa found out and told me I had the most gorgeous complexion in the whole world, to never be ashamed of it. 'What's wrong with being black or brown or coffee-coloured?' he roared. 'What do your young *chiku* friends know?' He called me Hitam Manis from then onwards. '*Hitam*' means 'black' and '*manis*' sweet, as you know. That's the Baba way of saying 'Black is Beautiful'. My nickname, Manis, has sort of stuck, I guess."

Manis' greatest passion was cooking. She cooked her dishes from memory, never once referring to a recipe book. Kai noticed that instead of using proper measuring cups or scales, Manis used ladles, spoons, bowls, coconut shells, even egg shells.

"How do you cook without a recipe, Aunty Manis? How do you know the quantity?" Kai asked in amazement, as she tossed a bowl of dried mushrooms and a handful of tamarind pieces into the *itik tim* soup, another of Kai's favourite, a delicious soup of duck and salted mustard, flavoured with white pepper corns and nutmeg.

"My dear boy, it's called *agak-agak*. In Baba Malay, it simply means to estimate, to 'guess guess'."

"You don't look like you're guessing. You look dead sure," he teased.

"*Ha ha* ... comes with years of practice. You just sort of know intuitively," chirped Manis as she expertly julienned thin slivers of kaffir lime leaves and torch ginger flower to garnish her prawn *kerabu* salad.

"No nyonya worth her salt will cook from a recipe book, at least not from my generation. I'm quite sure the next generation will be different — my two daughters don't even know how to cook rice or fry an egg!" she exclaimed.

"I tell them this is your heritage, you must at least try to learn a dish or two, but they tell me, 'No time, No time-lah', or 'Not interested'," she sighed. "They are both so occupied with their careers and their corporate world."

"They're lucky they have you," Kai said wistfully.

"Well, I'm not going to be around forever. What if I die tomorrow? All this will be gone, all this knowledge. All these dishes passed down through the generations ... from my great, great grandma down to me ... two girls and both not interested," she lamented and shook her head.

"My second daughter doesn't even know how to boil a kettle of water or where the kettle is kept!" she laughed, "But I can't complain, I guess. They're both very successful and ambitious, climbing that ridiculous ... what-you-call-it ... *ah* yes the corporate ladder. When they reach the top, they're going to find there's nothing up there."

"I do wish sometimes, just sometimes, they'd come into the kitchen and hang out with me, like the way you do, Kai," she added.

Kai picked up a young kaffir lime leaf and breathed in its delicate scent. Manis finished slicing the remaining leaves and flowers. Kai helped her sprinkle the fine pink and green slivers all over the salad.

"Wow, it looks too good to eat now!" Kai exclaimed.

Manis noted, "At least you're interested, Kai. I'll teach you. Maybe you can teach my girls some day when I'm gone. Charge them 300 dollars an hour ... *Hee hee*," chuckled Manis.

"*Ahh*, I know what to do … Kai, since you're so keen, I'll teach you how to cook my dishes, share all the secrets of nyonya cooking with you, how about that?"

"That is simply super, Aunty Manis," grinned Kai as he slurped down a bowl of the scrumptious *itik tim* soup.

The next morning, Kai was in the kitchen making a cup of tea, sniffing the air, trying to guess what Manis was cooking that day.

How odd.

There was just the smell of rubber. No smells at all emanating from next door. Nothing except for that infernal rubber. There weren't any sounds either. No clang of a pot, chop-chop of shallots, no strains of a golden oldie wafting across on the morning breeze.

The silence was howlingly loud. He went out to the backyard and yelled,

"Aunty Manis, are you okay? It's pretty quiet. Is everything alright?"

No response.

Kai sensed something was wrong. He had never encountered such an ominous silence. He dropped his cup of tea and ran over to Manis' house. The front door was open, everything was strangely still. He looked everywhere, the kitchen, the bedrooms, bathrooms, but she was nowhere to be seen. Kai ran back into the kitchen looking for some signs.

A bowl of naked shallots and garlic pips sat quietly on the kitchen table. A half cup of coffee was beside it, still warm.

Kai noticed the back door was slightly ajar. He pushed it open and stepped out into the back yard. He had been out here a few times to pluck pandan or curry *pillai* leaves from Manis' luxuriant herb garden. It was quite large with a steep slope behind. The familiar clumps of galangal and pandan, the beds of *daun kesom, cekur* and lemongrass, the pots of basil and mint, the wild *daun kadok* creeping rampantly into the moss-covered drain, the exotic *bunga kantan* or ginger flower protruding from the mass of shiny green leaves, the creeping *bunga telang* with its bright blue flowers which Manis used to colour the glutinous rice, Kai ran to every corner looking desperately for her.

He found her sprawled on the grass beside the mango tree, a pair of kitchen scissors clasped tightly in her hand. He knelt down beside her and felt her pulse — it was very faint. Swiftly, Kai lifted her up in his arms. Struggling and panting, he carried her into the house, placed her on the sofa, then called the ambulance. He found a piece of paper with her husband's and daughters' telephone numbers stuck on the fridge with a magnet in the shape of a wok. He called them to give the news.

Then, he sat beside her, holding her hand, praying with all his heart, shivering with fear for her safety.

"Please please Aunty Manis, say you're alright. Please don't go, please don't leave us. Don't leave me, you are my friend, my very best friend."

She lay there, unconscious, not a sound, not a whisper.

By the time the ambulance arrived, her family members had all reached home and they accompanied her to the hospital.

Kai walked slowly back to his house. Back to his deathly quiet, rubber-smelling house. He glared at the pile of slippers, gave it a kick and watched the pile come tumbling down. He sat there amidst the slippers, waiting. The choking smell of rubber everywhere was suffocating.

An hour later, the phone rang. It was from one of Manis' daughters.

"Thank you for informing me. Sorry, I'm so sorry," Kai responded in a daze.

He put down the phone. He went to the kitchen to get a glass of water. He breathed in deeply, trying to imagine the friendly aroma of curries and sambals, the scent of leaves, flowers, fruits and vegetables being cooked, pounded, sliced, the sounds of laughter and song, the music of pots, pans and knives.

Just the overpowering smell of rubber, and a cruel silence.

With no daughters to cook, he knew there would be no more smells and noises.

A vintage sarong with motifs of roosters and fans in the background.

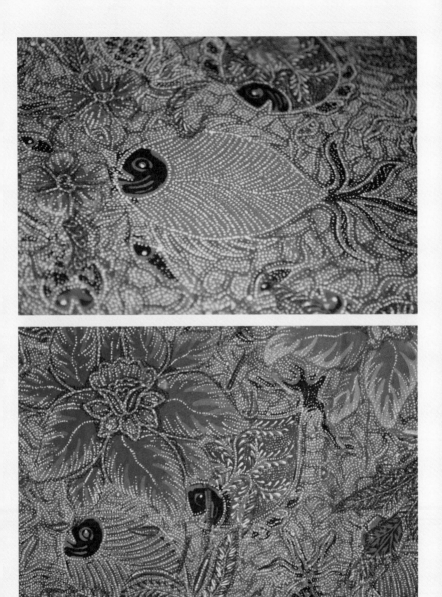

An eighty-year-old sarong with motifs of fish swimming amidst a floral fantasy.

Two dragon fishes from a forty-year-old Pekalongan sarong. Fishes are regarded as bearers of good fortune and wealth.

A peacock (top) and a rooster (bottom). Peacocks are symbols of beauty while roosters are believed to repel evil spirits. (Courtesy of Baba Lee Yuen Thein)

BABA IDIOMS

Monyet kena belachan

*(Translation: A monkey who has
just tasted sambal belachan)*
*Meaning: Someone who is extremely restless,
in a state of panic.*

Monyet pakai manek-manek

(Translation: A monkey dressed in chains of beads)
Meaning: An incorrigible show-off

Freedom in a Cage

Her heart softened at the tiny ball of fluff, its limbs scrawny as sticks. When it opened its eyes, they were the largest she'd ever seen, puffy eye bags and wrinkly skin beneath. It grabbed her finger, peeped shyly up at her from pinkish blue-veined eyelids and straightaway, Sue Lin was besotted with the tiny macaque.

Awek and Andak, two *orang asli* brothers living in the village nearby, had found it in one of their traps for wild boar. The baby monkey was trapped inside the bamboo cage, one limb bleeding from a nasty wound, whimpering in pain. They were reluctant to abandon it in the forest. They knew the monkey would never be accepted by its family once in contact with the human world. Its chances of survival were practically nil if left out in the wild — either killed by wild beasts or, worse, ending up in someone's cooking pot. Its only hope would be adoption by someone who loved animals and would care for it. Both brothers had someone in mind.

Just two weeks ago, they had met a couple who lived a short distance away in the same forest. This couple had decided to quit the rat race, bought a piece of land at the edge of the rainforest on the road to Fraser's Hill, a hill resort built during British colonial rule. Tucked away in a quiet valley with a view of the distant hills, the house was built of wood, perched solidly on stilts. It was a large and roomy space with a high ceiling. Its wide verandahs faced jungle-clad hills on one side, and two streams tumbling over rocks and giant boulders in an incessant, joyous melody on the other.

That day, Awek and Andak had collected two large wicker baskets of durians from deep in the forest. The entire night long, the wild durians fell, crashing through canopies of thick branches and leaves onto the ground below. It was a windfall. The brothers collected as many as they could, and the next morning, instead of heading to town to sell the fruits, they decided to try and sell the durians to the couple living nearby. They had no idea if they would be welcomed or not but decided to try their luck.

They cycled along the driveway leading to the couple's house, a basket of durians strapped to each bicycle. As they neared the house, located on a slight hill across the streams, they were shocked to see a pack of dogs charging down the steps, bounding across the bridge towards them, barking ferociously. Terrified, they jumped off their bicycles, dashed to the nearest trees and scrambled up the trunks.

The pitiful cries of '*Tolong, tolong!*' and the ruckus raised by the dogs brought the couple, Joe and Sue Lin, rushing out of the house. They saw two pairs of brown arms and legs clinging to two tree trunks for dear life. On closer inspection, they saw two terrified pairs of eyes looking down at the dogs, growling and snapping at their heels. The dogs were just toothless tigers, one yell from their master Joe and they started wagging their tails in a friendly manner. Awek and Andak were coaxed down and invited into the house. They were served coffee by three *orang asli* girls from the village nearby, who worked part-time for Sue Lin. Joe felt bad for the two shaken nervous *orang asli* and bought all the durians from them.

The couple, Awek and Andak noticed, had no children but a menagerie — an assortment of pedigree Bull Mastiffs, bulldogs and pariahs. A few cats lolled about the house in a love-hate existence with the dogs, from hissing and swatting their tender noses with their sharp claws to preening and purring. Outside the house, in a fenced compound were a gaggle of geese munching salads of fresh lettuce and spinach. Running or waddling all over the land and beneath the house were chickens, roosters, ducks, even a pair of turkeys! The two brothers left happy with the money Joe gave them for the durians and touched by the kindness of Sue Lin and Joe.

When they found the monkey, Awek and Andak did not waste any more time deliberating over it. There was a home waiting, they were sure of it. Joe and Sue Lin would take him in. They put the monkey in a gunny sack and cycled immediately to their house. Sure enough, it didn't take long to convince them to take in the orphaned monkey.

"Let's keep it. He will be killed if we throw him back into the forest," said Sue Lin, gently cuddling the monkey.

"Guess one more animal won't cause any harm," Joe agreed.

The *orang asli* brothers were pleased the couple had agreed to take in the monkey. Just before they left though, they warned Joe and Sue Lin it was a wild animal and they must release it into the jungle when it grew older.

"*Sekarang kecik, comel. Nanti besar, jaga,*" Awek and Andak advised in Malay and cycled away, waving at the dogs who wagged their tails in return.

Sue Lin and Joe loved the little monkey. It had a cheeky smile and a tuft of hair on top of its head and was given the name of Cherokee after a Native American tribe, or Cheko for short. He was pampered with generous portions of delicious foods from the kitchen. Every morning, he enjoyed a breakfast of *nasi lemak* and fruits. When Sue Lin and Joe went to bathe in the stream, Cheko accompanied them. Sometimes, Joe would take Cheko for a walk in the forest. Unleashed, Cheko was carefree, clambering up the trees, jumping from branch to branch, following Joe faithfully, his eyes always trained on his master. With all the opportunities for escape, he never did. He was wary of the jungle with its strange noises and unseen dangers.

As he grew bigger and stronger, Sue Lin and Joe tried to return Cheko back into the wild. Once, they walked quite a distance into the forest with him tied to a long leash. Upwards, past three tiers of waterfalls, they climbed with the unsuspecting Cheko bounding alongside them. Finally they reached a site where they felt it would be safe to release the macaque. He scrambled about busily exploring the area, oblivious to his impending fate. Joe and Sue Lin watched Cheko darting about in the foliage above. Joe whispered, "This is our chance, Sue Lin. He's not looking. Let's go! Quick!"

They turned and stealthily crept away.

Within a few minutes, they heard a loud screeching above them. It was Cheko. He was screaming at them. He followed them closely as they walked home, scolding non-stop, chattering angrily. Sue Lin and Joe tried to persuade Cheko not to follow them but it hovered above, jumping from branch to branch till they reached home. There, he scampered back to his cage, scratching himself nervously, still screeching his disgust at being dumped by his 'parents'.

They tried several times again to release Cheko but never succeeded. Cheko would watch them like a hawk, never straying too far away. Finally, resigned, they decided to wait and see, hoping that he would not pose any danger to anyone. He had been reared by humans from infancy, surely he could reside in peace with humans.

As the years passed by, Cheko grew even bigger, no longer the helpless creature that had captured Sue Lin's heart. His huge thighs were muscular, his torso broad as a boxer's chest. He had become mean and ferocious and enjoyed scaring anyone he disliked. He only respected his master Joe. Even his reaction to his mistress depended on his moods, the rest he enjoyed frightening the living daylights out of them. Whenever anyone came to peer at him in his cage, he would pretend to look nonchalant, even force his mouth into an artificial silly smile, scratching himself vigorously. When the visitor relaxed and came nearer, he would jump with all his strength, hitting the wire cage with a thump, snarling ferociously. The visitor would usually run screaming back to the house, which suited Cheko fine as he despised being the object of stares and stupid comments like, 'Hi Monkey', 'Hello Monkey' or worse, 'Hi, Ugly'.

Heh heh heh ... i so clever ... scare you man ... you wee-wee yos trousers ... ha ha ... so stoopid ... wan come close like velly clever ...

Cheko now lived in a spacious cage at the back of the house, with a tyre to swing on, a wooden shelter, and a fibre-glass pool of fresh water. Joe had gotten his contractor to build this comfortable den as he was worried at the speed Cheko was growing and his powerful strength.

The three *orang asli* maids were getting more nervous by the day. The oldest, Along, voiced her anxiety to Sue Lin one evening after she had just fed Cheko, "Aunty, Cheko *sudah masuk angin. Gila. Nanti keluar, habis kita semua!*"

Sue Lin discussed this with Joe that night, "I'm worried. Along says Cheko is moody, crazy. If he escapes, we are done for, *kaput!*"

"We'll just have to make sure the cage is stronger. I'll call Ah Tuck tomorrow."

Even Si-Gemok, the gardener who loved boasting of his blowpipe skills, muttered in his broken English, "*Monyet* you too biggy. No goody. Come out die! *Mampus*," he mumbled while Cheko glared, twitching his thick eyebrows up and down, then jumped onto the wall of the cage, creating a dent in the thick wire mesh. Si-Gemok pulled back in fright, turned and waddled away.

Hissssss ... Go away Fatso! So gemok ... cannot even run ... Bite yos fat backside, you know...

All the fears of the household were not totally unfounded, for one day, it really happened.

It came to pass when some visitors came to stay at Sue Lin's country home.

Sue May, Sue Lin's younger sister, arrived with her young son, Jeremy, and two friends, one from Britain and the other from New Zealand, for a short holiday in the country retreat. The first day was spent playing in the streams, feasting on durians and delicious home-cooked food and walks in the forest. After dinner they gathered on the verandah for drinks. Joe was a whisky man and enjoyed sharing his fascinating collection of whiskies and liqueurs neatly laid out on a table beside the verandah. They swapped stories and travel adventures, chatting way past midnight, enjoying the singing of the cicadas, and the cool temperature.

The next morning, Jeremy offered to feed Cheko. Excitedly, he trudged to Cheko's den at the back of the house with a packet of *nasi lemak*. His aunt called out to remind him, "Don't forget to lock the latch of the small window. That's where you feed him. Through that little window. Do not open the door."

"Okay," Jeremy replied.

When he approached the cage, he was surprised to see Cheko had grown tremendously, almost his size.

"Hi Cheko, remember me? You've really grown. I can't recognise you."

Cheko was pacing up and down the length of his cage. He suddenly sat down on the cement floor and started scratching himself, eyes half-closed, his bright red penis sticking out obscenely.

Wait come ... closer ... nearer... come city boy ... I can see you ... heh heh you tink I no see you ... tink I scratching like a monkey ...

Quietly Jeremy crept up to the cage, unlocked the latch of the window, opened it slightly and tried to toss in the packet of *nasi lemak*. With one leap, Cheko pounced on the ledge beneath the window hissing terrifying noises and grabbed Jeremy's hand. Jeremy pulled his hand out just in time. Terrified, he ran back to the main house, forgetting to lock the bolt of the window of Cheko's cage.

Ha ha so funny ... he scare till pucat ... OOOH he no lock back ... ha ha ... velly easy man ... i gotta stretch ... open big door ... Got It!

Soon, Jeremy was playing with the dogs and had forgotten the scary episode with Cheko. The two expat friends, Nigel the Brit and Sam the Kiwi, were relaxing on the sunny verandah. Sam was reading while Nigel was enjoying the lovely view of the streams. Butterflies in vivid hues fluttered about. Down by the streams, green and red dragonflies buzzed drowsily above shallow, sun-dappled pools.

Nigel noticed a monkey running beside the stream right below the house.

"Oh look! There's a monkey down below. All alone, strange ... They usually travel in packs ... this fellow is all by himse..."

Before he could finish his sentence, Cheko sprang with one mighty jump and landed on the balcony. Startled at the sight of the two strangers, it hissed loudly at the two men and bared its deadly yellowish teeth. It was a frightening sight — its teeth were long, vampire-like sticking out of a mouth drooling with saliva. Sam sprang up from his cosy rattan chair staring at it in horror, Nigel pressed himself against the wall, both men were speechless with shock.

The maids screamed, '*Jah, Jah*' and ran to the back of the kitchen, cowering in terror, grabbing kitchen mops and brooms for defence. All the dogs including the huge bull mastiffs crawled under the chairs and tables, whining and cringing. Joe had gone to the city for some business and Sue Lin had just driven off with her sister Sue May and nephew to the local market. The two expats realised it was just them and the monkey.

Cheko sat on the balcony, eyeing the two strangers, lifting its thick eyebrows and baring its teeth, the tuft of hair on its head sticking upright like a battle cry. Nigel ran to the kitchen and came back with two pot covers. He started banging them together.

"Noise, Sam, make a lot of noise! I know, I lived in South Africa before — the baboons hate noise."

"Shoo. Go away. Shoo!" they both shouted at the top of their voices.

The noise infuriated Cheko. He screeched in a high-pitched shattering tone, shat a huge pile of poo, then sprung off the bannister, landing with a thud on the verandah right in front of them!

"*Aaaiieee!*" the maids screamed, scuttling into the guest room located just behind the kitchen, followed by the dogs yelping with fear, tails between their legs.

"Oh damn, it doesn't work!" groaned Nigel.

"You sure they weren't scaring away the eclipse?" asked Sam.

"*Yeeech*, it stinks to high heaven," shrieked Nigel.

At the corner of his eye, Sam noticed Joe's precious whisky bottles on the low table in the front hall.

"Oh no, Joe's precious bottles!" gasped Sam, "We've got to save Joe's whiskies!"

"This pot banging isn't working! This hairy ape's taking it as a personal challenge!" Nigel threw the pot covers on the floor with disgust.

"I've an idea! Remember the movie *The Gods Must Be Crazy?* It's all about size. Grab a chair, Nigel! Do a Desmond Morris, show this ugly critter we're taller, bigger than him! Alpha male time!" shouted Sam.

They both grabbed hold of a chair, held it up above their heads and advanced towards Cheko with menacing looks imitating the monkey's snarls and hisses.

Ha ha look ... look ... funny white fellas ... putting chair on head ... you sit on them stupids ... even I knows

All hell broke loose. Cheko unleashed his fury to the fullest. Shrieking and snarling, he leaped all over the house. It was unbelievable how high and how far he could jump. His powerful legs propelled him upwards and he landed on a beam in the ceiling. Another mighty leap and he was in the front hall, one more jump and he landed right in front of them again.

"Yikes! The monster's back — right in front of us!" yelled Nigel still clutching the chair on top of his head.

"It doesn't work! He's not a normal monkey, he thinks he's human!" muttered Sam.

"Good lord, look at those fangs. If he sinks them into us, we're dead meat!" gasped Nigel.

Cheko raised himself to his full height, stuck out his chest and growled, frothing saliva. He was a terrifying sight. Just when they thought he was going to attack, with another gigantic leap, he landed on the kitchen table. He grabbed the bowl of fruits and stuffed fruit greedily into his mouth. He did not stay still for long. He was enjoying his reign of terror leaping around pissing and defecating everywhere, spitting pieces of fruit, breaking and smashing things in his way.

"Shall we hide in the guest room like the rest of them? I don't fancy the prospect of wrestling with this half-crazed ape!" asked Nigel queasily.

Crashhh! Cheko grabbed a dark green bottle from the table and smashed it on the floor.

"Oh damn! There goes Joe's rare eighteen-year-old Islay single malt..." spluttered Sam.

Another crash.

"And the rare schnapps from Slovakia..." Nigel continued mournfully.

Sam noticed a laundry basket full of clothes lying on the floor dumped by the maids in their haste to get away.

"Ahh, I have another idea!" exclaimed Sam.

Sam picked a fire engine-red sarong from the basket, ran to the nearest window and started waving and twirling it matador-style, taunting Cheko, "Come on you fat smelly thing. Come and get me! Ole! C'mon, El Toro..."

"Sam, what are you doing?" Nigel asked.

"Psssss ... here's hoping the creature will charge the red sarong and fall out of the window."

Cheko stopped smashing the bottles and eyed Sam momentarily.

Oi ... this gila white fella ... wat doing .. .doin wat ... flap-flap ... somemore my mistress sarong ...

Cheko's face contorted into a grin. He aimed a kiwi fruit at Sam before continuing wrecking the house. The whole place was a mess of stinking excrement, urine, broken bottles, glass shards, pieces of fruit and banana skins.

"Ouch, blinking idiot," growled Sam removing pieces of greenish fruit from his face, "This is bad, this is really bad. We'd better think of something fast!"

As if on cue, Along suddenly emerged from the guest room waving a banana in her hand. She called out the way she usually did when she fed Cheko every day.

"Cheko, here, Cheko, here," she purred in a shaky voice.

Cheko stopped his orgy of smashing bottles, glasses, plates and perked up listening to the familiar voice.

Aehh? Ya kah? Feeding time awredi ah?

Cheko turned in the direction of her voice and saw her standing just outside the bathroom between the kitchen and the guest room. He started bounding towards her.

Screaming as Cheko charged towards her, she tossed the banana into the bathroom.

Cheko leapt into the bathroom after the banana. Along quickly slammed the bathroom door after him.

"Bravo! Bravo!" cheered Sam and Nigel, "Clever girl!"

Along grinned, muttering, "*Sengoh, sengoh,*" in her Semai language.

"Problem solved for the moment," Sam added.

"Huh? What do you mean 'for the moment'?" Nigel asked.

"Don't you remember? The bathroom door opens from the inside. There's no lock from the outside. This means he's not locked in."

"Gaaa...but...but he doesn't know that, right? He's just a monkey."

"Let's hope so."

Oi ... wowee ... many toys here ... splash splash ... play play lah ... Eeeek ... who this ... ugly ugly tink ... behind glass

Meanwhile Sue Lin was speeding home after a desperate call from Along and the news that Cheko was terrorising the entire household. Sue Lin knew that no one could control Cheko except Joe, but he was too far away. Who to call for help? The police, the Fire Brigade or the Wildlife Department? She called her vet.

"Dr Vijay, help! What am I to do? My monkey has escaped!"

"Where? Back into the jungle?" asked the animal doctor.

"No, he's creating havoc in the house. It's impossible to catch him — he's huge and ferocious!"

"Can't your *orang asli* folks knock him out with their blowpipes?"

"They've lost the art. It's called progress."

"Try valium then. That should work."

"What? Valium?"

"Yes, tranquillisers. Knock him out then bundle him back into his cage."

"Brilliant idea. But ... how to give valium to a monkey?"

"Break it into pieces, hide it inside some food and give it to him, he won't know."

Sue Lin drove at top speed to the doctor's clinic in town, charged in, grabbed the tranquilisers from the counter and charged out again.

When they arrived home, it was like a war zone. Everyone was standing near the bathroom, looking solemn and anxious.

"Where's Cheko?" Sue Lin asked worriedly.

"*Dalam sini.* Here," responded Along pointing to the bathroom.

"She threw in a banana and the greedy fella jumped in," Sam explained.

"Quick, Along, get me some bread," ordered Sue Lin.

She whipped out the valium from her handbag, crushed them into small pieces and slipped the valium inside some slices of bread. Opening the bathroom door slightly, she threw in the pieces of bread then slammed the door shut again.

"Aaah, that should do it. Now all we've got to do is wait for the tranquilliser to work," exclaimed Sue Lin, looking relieved.

Some semblance of normalcy returned – the dogs were let out of the guest room and sent outside, the *orang asli* girls started cleaning up the mess.

The rest stood beside the bathroom door listening to Cheko. He was on a rampage. They could hear him throwing buckets, tissue rolls, bottles, tooth brushes and tooth paste tubes all over the room. Suddenly, a piercing screech followed by more things thrown angrily around.

"He's probably seen his reflection in the mirror!" Sue Lin guessed.

"Doesn't like what he sees, obviously," chortled Nigel.

"How do we know if he's swallowed the valium?" asked Sam.

"He's a greedy guy ... he'll eat anything. Just have to wait," assured Sue Lin.

They sat around the kitchen table waiting for the commotion to stop. After thirty minutes, everything fell silent.

"It's gone quiet. Is he tranquilised you think ... or just resting?" asked Sue May.

"I'm quite sure he's knocked out," said Sue Lin.

"Err ... don't mean to spoil the show but I just remembered monkeys don't necessarily consume everything, they keep extra food in their pouches in their mouths ... Arrrrgggghh! He's back!!!" screamed Nigel.

All heads turned and there just outside the bathroom standing upright on his thick haunches grinning and baring his teeth was Cheko.

They screamed in terror and jumped to their feet.

Sue Lin tried to calm him, "Hi Cheko, Cheko, good boy."

Cheko scratched under both his armpits not quite sure what to do.

Aiya ... boring ... life so boring ... nutting to do ... i fedup play in jamban ...

He opened his mouth and yawned, revealing his repulsive fangs.

It was surreal, almost a repeat — the dogs who had returned to the house yelped and crawled under the few tables left upright, the *orang asli* girls screamed hysterically, dropped their brooms and mops and ran out of the house.

Sue Lin and family stood transfixed, gaping at Cheko. Sam quietly opened a kitchen drawer and grabbed the kitchen knife, clutching it behind his back.

"Good heavens, he *does* know how to open the door. Bloody clever!" gasped Nigel.

But Cheko was fed up and tired. He missed his cosy den and his soft bed. All the excitement had worn him out. He jumped out of the window, bounded to his cage and sat quietly inside.

Ahhh home ... goody goody ... wah that ting ... in jamban mirror ... yech ugly ugly ...

"Huh? Where'd he go?" Sue Lin gasped, "he just jumped out!"

They heard a shout from Along out at the back yard.

"Aunty aunty, *dia sudah balik. Balik rumah dia! Saya sudah kunci dia dalam.*"

"Oh thank heavens, he's gone back to his cage! Along has locked the cage after him," Sue Lin muttered with relief.

"What? I don't believe it! How strange," gasped Nigel.

"All's well that ends well then, except for some very good whiskies," mourned Sam.

For almost a year after that, Joe and Sue Lin tried every place they could think of. They called up the wildlife department but didn't get any assistance, they called several zoos but were told they already had plenty of macaques. No one wanted Cheko. They had no heart to put him down and continued to keep him as a pet, or rather as a temperamental, foulmouthed relative whom no one wanted.

As the years passed, Cheko kept growing bigger and bigger. And meaner and crankier. All the *orang asli* living in the village nearby knew or had heard of the ferocious monkey and till today shudder at the thought of it breaking loose one day. Perhaps it's a good thing for they've taken up practising their blowpipe skills again.

Apart from that, *ssshhhhhh* ... it's a secret, no one, absolutely no one else knows.

A contemporary batik sarong from Cirebon, featuring mythical animals borrowed from Hindu, Muslim and Chinese mythology.

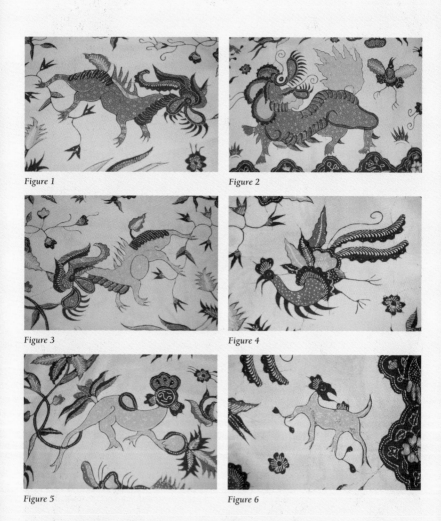

Figure 1

Figure 2

Figure 3

Figure 4

Figure 5

Figure 6

Figures 1, 2 and 3 could be either a Kilin (Qilin) or the Singa Putih, originally the white lion, the symbol of the kingdom of Pajajaran. A mythological creature with the body of a deer, skin with scales of a goldfish and head of a dragon, it symbolises truth and justice. Figure 4 looks like a hong bird, or a phoenix. Figure 5 is the Bouraq, a half-human, half-bird figure sometimes found in Arabic calligraphy. Figure 6 looks like a deer.

The Tenant Upstairs

"Stop it! Stop! Mama, what are you doing?" screamed Diana, trying to push her mother away.

"Sit still, stop struggling. There's no time to waste. They're coming! They're coming!" snapped her mother, her voice cold as icy steel.

She clutched her daughter's right arm and held her down forcefully on the chair, maniacally snipping off Diana's gorgeous, tumbling tresses with her kitchen scissors.

Diana protested as her hair rained on the floor,

"Why, Mama? Why?" her tears falling as her hair was shorn violently off her head.

"Cry all you like, Diana. I'll explain later. Now quick, take off your top."

Diana sensed her mother's frantic urgency and obeyed. She caught a glimpse of herself in the Venetian mirror and gasped, "*Owwww*, why do you have to cut it this way? Can't you do it nicer, Mama? I look ghastly!" she bawled recoiling from her reflection, a horrible haircut with untidy, jagged edges.

"The uglier the better," asserted her mother.

Her mother cut a long strip of cloth from her *kain lepas* sarong, a beautiful piece of *batik* from Jogjakarta which she loved.

"Mama, that's your favourite sarong!'

"I've got no time to look for a length of cloth. This will do. Here, wear this — it will protect you."

She pulled her daughter towards her and wrapped the cloth around her daughter's chest, pulling it tight till her breasts were pushed flat against her body. After wrapping the cloth around Diana's chest a few times, she fastened two ends of the cloth together in a tiny knot.

"Don't take it off, you understand? Only when you bathe. From now on you are a boy, understand?"

"What? I don't want to be a boy!"

"Put this on, hurry!" she commanded giving Diana a baggy shirt belonging to her elder brother and a pair of black cotton pants.

Diana did not protest anymore sensing something wrong and that her mother was trying to protect her. She had just turned fourteen, blossoming into a young delicate beauty, with a curvaceous figure and thick dark hair that cascaded down her shoulders.

As Diana hurriedly dressed in the boy's attire, her mother May Joon watched, pale and tense.

"Oh God, *tolong Tuhan*, please, please protect her. I should have done this earlier, Diana. But ... but I didn't have the heart ... I wanted to give you a few more days ... of life as a girl," her mother said.

She rushed out to the kitchen and returned with a piece of charcoal. She smeared Diana's face, neck, hands, palms. She surveyed her work, still critical even though Diana now resembled a dirty, unkempt street urchin.

"Mama, how can I live like this?"

"You must. You have to if you want to survive."

"Life is already tough under the Japanese Occupation, Mama. No school, no friends, not enough food, and now this ... this awful disguise. Why?"

She pulled her daughter close to her bosom, surprising her with a gentle hug and a kiss on her forehead. Holding Diana close, she explained her actions to her bewildered daughter.

"Hock Kwee, our neighbour, just came by on his bicycle to warn me that the Japs are coming! They are searching from house to house along our street, looking for young girls, women..."

"What are they after?" Diana looked puzzled.

"After ... err ... well, if they find you, they will ... will rape you, take you away to their brothels, or kill you after they are done with you."

"What about you, Ma? Aren't you in danger too?"

May Joon continued, her voice steely and determined, "It's you I'm concerned about. From now on, you are a boy, a servant boy. Get away from here as fast as you can. Make your way to Aunty Lina's house. If the Japs catch you, pretend to be an idiot, you hear me? Drool, act stupid, retarded.

"I should have sent you away earlier to Uncle Seong's in the *ulus* when there was still a chance ... but you're all I have. They've taken away your brother. And your Papa ... he has not come home for weeks ... I don't know where he's gone..." her tough demeanour cracked. She brushed her tears angrily away, grabbed Diana's hand and rushed her to the back of the house.

Opening the heavy timber door, she whispered, "Now go, quickly, keep very quiet. I will come and look for you when it's safe. Go, my dearest, run."

"Mama, please ... I am scared." Diana pleaded as the blackness of the night enveloped her.

"No more words, daughter. Be brave."

Diana took a last glance at her mother standing at the door, silhouetted against the warm yellow light of the kitchen, strands of hair trailing out from her dishevelled *sanggul*, her face haggard with worry and sorrow. She looked frail as a leaf in a raging storm but her indomitable spirit gave Diana strength. Pressing a goodbye kiss on her lips to her mother, she slipped silently into the gloomy shadows.

May Joon was left alone in the big empty house. She had to stay and pretend all was normal, deflect the Japs from searching for her daughter. Collaborators might have already done their foul work, pointing out the homes where families with young daughters lived. She snatched family portraits from the dresser and threw them in a drawer, swept away the fallen hair.

Suddenly, she remembered she had a tenant living upstairs. She abhorred that loud vulgar woman. Still, she felt duty-bound to warn her. Running to the top of the stairs, she yelled, "Rose, Rose, are you there? The Japanese soldiers are coming. They're going from door to door. Hurry, get out now!"

There was no sound. She walked along the dim corridor to the tenant's room and tried to open it. It was locked.

"Rose, Rose, can you hear me? Get out fast, Rose. The Japs are almost here!"

All was quiet.

Maybe she's gone out, thought May Joon, she always goes out late at night and returns the next morning. She remembered the tenant mentioning she worked 'night shifts' to Kong Beng, May Joon's husband. She sure doesn't look like a nurse with those high heels and low-cut tacky clothes, May Joon had commented sarcastically.

She heard a muffled sound from the room, then the low-pitched booming voice of her tenant, "Let the %#$@ shits come *lah* ... I'm not scared of those bow-legged scumbags. I'm not about to move my butt for anyone, least of all those smelly farts. Now get lost, Bossy. And stop your damn screeching. I'm not deaf!" Rose hollered.

"Go wash your foul mouth with chili powder! *Pergi mampus!*" May Joon retorted, turned and stormed downstairs.

Ingrate! May Joon fumed. I told him I don't trust this woman when she came around looking for a room to rent. Coarse, foul-mouthed, *betul-betul kasar*. The way she stuck out her boobs at Kong Beng simpering, pleading for a place to stay. Once she started to use her tears on him, he was a goner. Soft-hearted husband of mine, so *lembek*, always being conned by people with sob stories.

"I can't turn down someone who needs help, May Joon. She's got nowhere to go. We have many spare rooms upstairs. Besides she's offered to pay rent, some extra income will be useful ... buy us some tea or sugar from the black market. She sounds desperate. Why can't we extend a bit of kindness to her?" Kong Beng had argued to her surprise.

Reluctantly, May Joon agreed on condition the tenant moved out to another place within six months.

"I've always believed that if you do good, goodness will come back to you, maybe not immediately, maybe even a few generations later, but it will ... somehow it will find you." Kong Beng clasped his wife's hand and gave it a gentle, reassuring squeeze.

What about you, Beng? Is anyone helping you? Are your kind deeds being returned? You've disappeared from the face of the earth. Probably dead or dying in a labour camp, she raged in abject bitterness as she slumped into a chair in the front hall waiting.

Angry, impatient fists pounded on the door accompanied by loud howls and guttural shouts.

May Joon clamped her mouth with her hand to smother a scream. They were here! Right outside her front door. She could smell their sweaty odour and worse, the smell of alcohol. She shrank against the wall, too frightened to move, her legs turning wobbly. She did not want to open the door. They would tear it down and kill her if she disobeyed. She had to stay alive for Diana's sake.

Two Japanese soldiers barged in clumsily the minute she opened the door. They were both drunk, reeling unsteadily, shouting, "*ku nian ku nian*," like hungry dogs on heat, licking their lips, poking, pushing her to bring out the maidens they craved. They were armed, rifles with bayonets and knives strapped around their waists.

She bowed low several times, her tiny, wiry body trembling with loathing and fear. She forced herself to appear calm, gesticulating there was no one else in the house, no girls.

"Don't have. No *ku nian*. No young girls. No one here. Only me, old caretaker. Everyone gone away," she articulated slowly, shaking her head and hands, not knowing if they could comprehend.

They looked astonished, played out. They started searching the house, at first giggling stupidly expecting to bump into virgins in every room, burping, belching from excessive food and drink. They searched the rooms downstairs, breaking things, smashing glasses and plates she'd left on the dish rack in the kitchen. They wobbled upstairs, the stairs creaking and protesting under their weight. She could hear them slamming doors violently. They came down looking more frustrated by the minute, peering behind the curtains, opening cupboards again.

May Joon knelt on the floor, bowing every time they came near.

They came out to the front hall, scratching their heads, barking at each other in staccato yells. The chubby one with the missing front teeth cursed, touching his crotch. The other soldier smashed the mirror angrily with the butt of his rifle, kicked and overturned a chair. They turned around and looked at the petite woman in the sarong kneeling, forehead on the floor, motionless, trying to evaporate from their sight.

Suddenly they attacked her. One soldier yanked her up and dragged her to the table. The other tore at her clothes, pulled her hair. She screamed and fought back, kicking, lashing out with every ounce of strength in her. She scratched their faces and necks with her fingernails, tried to gouge their eyes. The chubby soldier yelped and slapped her hard, stunning her momentarily. She screeched at the top of her voice, scratched again and pummelled with her fists.

They were too strong for her. They were both laughing and giggling hysterically. One soldier pinned her down on top of the table, leaned over and bit her viciously on her neck, her ear. The chubby one, drooling with saliva, punched her, pawed her thighs, and tried to pull her legs apart. Lurching unsteadily, he reached out to unzip his fly and was about to climb on the table and on top of her when he suddenly stopped at the sound of a woman's low, husky voice.

"Hello darlings, whatever are you doing with that skinny old goat? I'm much prettier any time. And I'm available..."

The two soldiers were taken by surprise. They had not found anyone in their search. The chubby one turned around fumbling for his dagger, while the other jerked upright, letting go of his victim.

They relaxed when they saw a shapely woman standing on the stairs, draping herself on the banister. They could not understand what she was saying but were mesmerised by her low breathy voice, every syllable enunciated caressingly and her suggestive body movements.

They stared at her gaping, blinking like little boys who had stumbled into a candy store.

Slowly, Rose, the foul-mouthed tenant whom May Joon despised, untangled herself tantalisingly from the banister, minced down the last three steps like a Japanese doll, put up both her hands, flapped them and muttered sexily, "Promise I won't scratch..."

She put one hand on the banister, the other on her hip and swivelled her hips like a striptease dancer, bumping and grinding, humming a little tune.

May Joon pulled herself up and crawled from the table to a corner of the room, away from the soldiers who had completely forgotten her, ogling the woman gyrating on the steps.

Rose wore a glittering, sequined crimson gown with a slit that went all the way up her right thigh. The tight bodice and low neckline revealed a well-endowed body that had seen better days and highlighted a flabby tummy. Strands of faux pearls dangled round her neck and a long strip of blue feathers fluttered around her sagging shoulders.

May Joon thought she looked like a nightmare but in the dark, spotlighted by a single naked bulb, she looked like a foxy vixen, shaking her shoulders, swinging her hips. The soldiers clapped, jabbering excitedly.

"C'mon fellas, let's go upstairs and play. Leave this scrawny, screechy crow alone," cooed Rose, still taking potshots at May Joon's expense, "... she doesn't like me, never did, never will."

May Joon slowly melted into the long curtains hanging over the French windows, trembling from the assault, wiping blood from her neck, her breasts, nursing soreness in every pore.

By now, Rose had figured the soldiers could not understand a word of English. Still swaying seductively, she sashayed up the stairs, waving a manicured finger at them, beckoning them to follow.

"C'mon, you slimy shits, follow me ... frankly, you make me puke ... but a girl's go to do what she's gotta do ... dumb nuts probably don't own a stinking dollar ... everything take for free ... s'okay ... conk out in a minute I can tell from your foul breath..." she smirked as they wobbled towards the stairs.

May Joon looked at them panting up the steep staircase after Rose. She held her face in horror, realising what the tenant was doing for her.

Rose stopped halfway up the stairs, her disgust and revulsion appearing in her eyes fleetingly, before she wiped it away with a smile. Like a pro, she purred, "Slowly fellas, don't fall all over me, you're ruining my dress, what's the hurry, you grinning apes?" then she raised her voice a little louder, "Hey, Bossypants, get out fast. When Humpy and Dumpy come down, you'd better be gone, just in case they want more on the menu. You hear me?"

May Joon tried to thank her but was silenced by Rose at the top of the stairs, "Not a word. Stay invisible. Now go. I'm not doing this for you, so don't thank me ... I'm just repaying a debt."

Quietly, May Joon hobbled out, shutting the door softly behind her.

A contemporary batik tulis *piece by Hartono Sumarsono in 2013. The phoenix is a symbol of grace and gentleness. The phoenix is yin, the female counterpart to the dragon (yang). Believed to ward off misfortune, it is a popular motif in Pekalongan sarongs.*

Maternal grandmother Swee Neo
watched protectively over her five
daughters during the Japanese Occupation.
My mother was 18 years old when Malaya
fell. Her sisters and she had to disguise
themselves as boys and were sent to live in
a remote area with a relative.

Right: My father fell in love with
the girl in a friend's photo album.
She was my mother posing
by a peacock flower tree.
They were married after
the end of World War II.

Wedding day of my parents, Mr and Mrs Lee Koon Liang.

The Collector

She watched him as he skillfully cut intricate patterns out of the *ang cho*, or red paper, with a pair of scissors and gently pressed them on top of the *kueh bakul*, sticky circular rice cakes wrapped in banana leaves, loved by the nyonyas for its gooey sweetness. His long fingers looked like a famous pianist's she'd seen on television – nimble, graceful, delicate. Deftly, he cut strips of *ang cho* in wavy patterns to decorate around the rice cakes and folded pieces of red paper into little triangles, making incisions in the folds. When spread open, the paper cuttings emerged as dainty, webbed circles of red which he used to adorn the plates of fruits and nyonya cakes.

The table was decorated beautifully for the ancestor worship ritual. He had started preparations weeks ago and awakened before dawn to cook the feast. Swathed in a red satin cloth with embroidered prancing lions in gold, the table and its contents looked like a banquet for the gods. Two brass candlesticks holding red candles were positioned on each side of a turquoise-green incense burner for holding joss sticks. Eight rice bowls and eight tiny cups of wine and tea with spoons and chopsticks to match sat in a row behind, neatly spaced. Favourite foods of his parents such as *ayam buah keluak*, *itik tim* and *lemak nenas* were offered together with the usual repertoire of curry chicken, *ayam pongteh*, *chap chye* and *hee piow* soup. Side dishes of *acar awak*, fried chicken, *sambal* prawns were served in matching plates.

She noticed he walked to the front of the table with a gentle reverence in his body movements, as if unseen guests were already present, surveying the offerings, ensuring nothing was forgotten. Satisfied, he lit the candles and joss sticks then knelt down to pray and to invite the spirits of his ancestors to partake of the meal he had cooked in their honour. She saw how his eyes sparkled when his relatives praised him for all the work and his delicious food. He loved playing host and took great pains to ensure the presentation was equally delightful and sumptuous as the feast.

She was relieved he took care of all these matters, she had no time nor interest in these peculiar baba-nyonya rituals he observed, but she did not complain. She enjoyed the amazingly complex and delicious feasts he cooked for special occasions, as long as she didn't have to get involved. They had been married for more than twelve years and there was hardly any disharmony in the marriage. He was a faithful and caring husband who took over all the responsibilities of running the household. Except Molly felt that something was missing, something was wrong but she couldn't place her finger on it.

She confided this to her close circle of girlfriends over lunch one day.

"What do you mean, Molly? He does everything for you, cooks, washes up, irons, even goes to the market, and earns an honest living. How many men will do all that? I'm envious of you. My husband won't lift a finger to help!'" exclaims Jessica.

"I know. I do appreciate that. He is a good friend, a companion. I enjoy talking with him and doing things together ... except ... except..."

"Except what? Is he not good in bed? He's not satisfying you?" queried the straight-talking, voluptuous Zainah, her buddy from school days.

"He's okay ... err ... I don't have anything to compare with."

"Is he cheating on you?" interrogated Zainah.

"No. Not that I know of. He comes home from his teaching job and goes straight to the kitchen to prepare the meal for the evening. I work till late, by the time I get home around eight, he's prepared a piping hot dinner, all laid out on the table."

"Lucky you! You have a 'wife'! It's every woman's secret dream ... What more do you want?" demands Ai Ling, looking up briefly from her incessant toying with her apps on her smart phone.

"I want ... I want ... I don't know ... yeah, guess I should count my blessings instead of complaining ... I'm not quite sure what I want," mused Molly.

Maybe she was jealous because he seemed to have so much energy and passion for life, she tried to rationalise. By the time she came home from her accountancy firm, she was exhausted, all she wanted to do was to kick off her shoes, have dinner and go to bed.

Richard would clean up after dinner. After throwing out the rubbish, tidying the house and plumping up the cushions on the sofa, he would disappear into his own world — going through his collections, documenting or reading to the music of golden oldies or his favourite *keroncong*.

He had an impressive collection of nyonya-ware which he loved showing off to his friends. Inside two gigantic rosewood cupboards he'd purchased from Malacca, were two magnificent coral-red and rich yellow porcelain *kam chengs*, circular tub-shaped containers, festooned with flowers and phoenixes, lions crouching on the top of their covers. A pair of rare brown *katmau* jars hogged the limited space with a set of lime green powder boxes used to store small tablets of *bedak sejuk* made of perfumed rice flour.

Next lay a breathtaking row of nyonya teapots in all kinds of shapes, sizes and colours. Besides these, he had inherited from his grandmother an entire rose-pink dinner set, complete with tureens, soup bowls, finger bowls, dinner and dessert plates, spoons, tea pots, milk jars and cups. Stunningly ornate, with its phoenixes, peonies and Buddhist symbols, it took pride of place on three shelves of the cupboard. On the bottom shelf, was a lovely collection of nyonya blue and white porcelain — batik bowls, spoons painted with roses, insects or birds, plates with fish, bats and butterfly designs, and sturdy bowls in a sweet pea design which he pulled out occasionally to use when he made *laksa* for his favoured guests.

The other cupboard was filled to overflowing with all kinds of bric-a-brac. Antique *kueh bangkit* wooden moulds competed for attention with *roti jala* and *kueh kapit* moulds. Gleaming brass candelabras, joss stick containers in peach and imperial yellow incense burners were kept together with tablecloths and covers in red satin exquisitely embroidered with lions and Chinese deities. A collection of *kasut manik*, or beaded slippers, worn by the nyonyas in the past occupied an entire shelf, with astounding designs of flamenco dancers, reindeer, roses, ribbons and bouquets on the panels, sewn laboriously by hand. Scores of silver belts with gigantic buckles festooned with flora and birds carried the secrets of the old nyonyas whose sarongs were kept decorously in place with their steely strength.

His collection of nyonya paraphernalia was not confined to the two cupboards. On top of the dresser, sideboards, sitting on carved wooden stands and plate holders were more *kam chengs*, cricket boxes and enchanting serving dishes with scalloped edges. On top of the book shelf in the second hall sat a row of *tengkat* or three-tiered enamel tiffin carriers in vibrant hues cosying up to antique *bakul siah*, or lacquered nyonya baskets, in black and red trimmed with gold.

In the kitchen was a collection of jade green chopstick holders and a blue and white *kam cheng* filled with fresh flowers. The lobby was graced with an antique red-gold bridal washstand where a Maiden Hair fern flourished in a terra cotta pot. Even the umbrella stand in the porch was a converted spittoon, and the unusual shaped flower pot was once a porcelain urinal used in the past by *bibiks* with loose bladders at night.

Sometimes, Molly felt like screaming, "*Arrrggggh* get rid of all these ridiculous hideous things! I hate clutter!"

She would have preferred a zen-like environment, everything in black and brown, with a sofa in black leather, so much easier to upkeep.

She complained about this to her girlfriends only to evoke responses like, "*Aiyooo* you don't want-*ah*, give me-*lah*!" exclaimed Ai Ling, "do you know how much these things cost now? A nyonya plate costs 6,000 ringgit nowadays ... prices have gone crazy."

"In Malacca, you cannot find authentic nyonya-ware anymore ... these Singaporeans *lah* with their mighty Singapore dollar, come and *sapu* everything. And now, guess who's next? The PRC! The rich Chinese from mainland China are coming to buy back everything old Chinese they can lay hands on..." added Ai Ling the financially savvy one.

"Smashed up a lot of things during their Cultural Revolution, didn't they?" pointed out Jessica.

Zainah said soothingly, "Molly-*ah*, your place is simply beautiful. I *suka*. Your husband really has that magic touch-*lah*, *Sayang*. You want to live in one of these leather and chrome minimalist settings, *meh*?"

"*Umm* well, yes actually! That would be a nice change. I mean c'mon, even in the toilet, he's got porcelain bowls with money plants! A toilet is a toilet."

Once Molly asked her husband, "Rich, what do you plan to do with all these things? We don't have any children, where's it all going to?"

He looked up at her astounded, holding his magnifying glass and carefully placed a small *kam cheng* in pale blue grey gently on the table as if it were a rare precious stone.

"What do you mean 'going to'?" he asked.

"Who's going to inherit all these? When we're both dead and gone!" Molly gesticulated dramatically at all the things around her.

"Oh, that's in the future," he smiled in his disarmingly charming way, "let's stay in the present."

Molly knew it was no point arguing because he was always calm and unruffled. He disliked engaging in arguments or shouting matches. She shrugged, stomped upstairs and went to sleep. No point waiting up for him anyway, she knew he would slip into bed way past midnight. He seldom initiated making love, not that she cared as he wasn't such a great lover anyway. It felt perfunctory, mechanical and he seemed distant, he seemed to be thinking, always thinking. Thinking of something else and it wasn't her.

One Sunday morning, he told her he was going to visit the weekend bazaar in Ampang, a suburb of Kuala Lumpur and asked politely if she wanted to come along.

She used to accompany him on his weekend jaunts to the various flea markets and garage sales in the city. Sometimes, they would drive all the way to Penang or Malacca on a tip-off from a dealer that an antique piece had arrived in the shop. Over the years, she seldom went along as she didn't share the same passion as Richard and got bored sitting in the musty shops amongst all the decaying old things.

But today she was in a good mood and said, "Yes, I don't mind coming along."

Again that sense of disquiet revisited her, that feeling of uncertainty. She noticed he looked startled, uneasy that she had accepted his invitation to join him.

He kept quiet in the car all the way to their destination. He looked troubled, examining his hands and fingernails every now and then whilst driving.

Molly touched his thigh gently and asked a question she had not asked for a long time, since courting days.

"Richard, do you love me?"

Five seconds of silence ensued before he gave her a cheerful, animated response, "Of course I do, Molly! Of course I love you. What a question to ask!"

He followed this by switching on the radio and hiking up the volume of his favourite channel, lapsing into silence again.

Am I going crazy? wondered Molly. It was just five seconds but in that time, the emptiness of words rang truer than his utterance of love.

The bazaar was teeming with vendors, hobbyists, collectors, tourists. Booths were filled to the brim with all kinds of things for sale ranging from old vinyl records, books, magazines, stamps, coins, clothes, jewellery, semi-precious stones, furniture, crockery to homemade cakes, pickles, jams and spices. Richard always went straight to his favourite section at the back of the vast hall where the genuine collectors milled around the several booths selling antiques and collectibles.

"Hey Richard, *apa macam?*" yelled Ariff manning a table cluttered with old Malay and nyonya jewellery, silver belts, wedding head dresses and decorative hair ornaments.

"*Baik.* I'm fine. *Apa khabar*, Ariff?" responded Richard, grinning with pleasure. He waved to him, then headed to his favourite booth owned by a Mr Tan. He sold all kinds of junk but occasionally, authentic nyonya-ware, getting them from his runners who scoured for antiques all over the country. Mr Tan spotted Richard from afar and gestured excitedly. When Richard and Molly reached his booth, Tan whispered to come over to his side of the table. Stealthily as though he had stolen the crown jewels, he pulled out a large parcel from a brown manila cardboard box and unwrapped the crumpled newspaper covering.

"*Ahhhh*, wow!" gasped Richard at the sight of a beautiful blue nyonya teapot emerging from the mess of grey and white newspapers.

"May I have a look at it please, Mr Tan?" he asked in a hushed tone.

Purring with pleasure, he lifted the teapot carefully from Mr Tan's hands.

"It's exquisite, simply exquisite!" Richard murmured stroking the side of the fat globular-shaped teapot lightly with his graceful fingers. It was a startling deep midnight blue, painted with sprays of peonies in famille rose, surrounded by petals and leaves in yellow and mauve. A pair of butterflies flitted on the teapot cover.

Mr Tan pulled out more treasures from the cardboard box — more nyonya plates, a light green tea tray with a cricket and chrysanthemums in the centre panel, a soap box in pale apricot.

"Genuine one, real one. See also you know, can tell what. Not repro I guarantee, you know I only sell the real stuff," Mr Tan assured them.

"Want or not? Quickly tell me. If you don't want, many people waiting only. You good customer, long-time customer, I give you first choice *lah*," he urged.

"Where did you find these, Mr Tan?' whispered Richard in amazement.

"My runner said from old nyonya in Malacca. Very sad *lor*, she emigrating to Australia. Her children say very fed up, cannot *tahan*, want to go to Melbourne so she also must pack up and go along. They all selling off their *barang*, furniture all gone. Now selling off their nyonya-ware."

"Very, very rare now, especially blue nyonya-ware," murmured Richard.

Richard spent a long time examining the porcelain pieces, scrutinising the reign marks at the bottom, examining them for any hairline cracks or tiny chips. He was especially besotted with the midnight blue teapot.

Molly waited impatiently. She felt pangs of hunger as she had only a cup of coffee for breakfast. She asked Richard to accompany her to the café downstairs for coffee and a snack.

"Molly, please, you go ahead. If I let go of these, someone else will come along and snap them up, no matter how much they cost. You go enjoy yourself, okay? You wait there. I'll come and join you as soon as I can. I'm going to try and persuade Mr Tan to give me a good price for the teapot."

It was very crowded in the little café. After her delicious meal of *nasi lemak* and a cup of coffee, she felt guilty occupying a seat when there were people waiting impatiently. Reluctantly she vacated her place and made her way up the stairs to the concourse to join Richard.

Walking towards the back portion of the hall, she saw someone with Richard. Hesitating, she tried to make out who it was. The person looked like a woman from afar, of medium height, slim, dressed in a pair of blue denim and a tie-dye teeshirt in orange and white swirls. Molly hurried forward a few more steps and hid behind a pillar.

Peeping out, she realised she was mistaken — it was a man absorbed in conversation with Richard who was still holding the teapot lovingly in his hands. His shoulder length jet-black hair was tied in a ponytail at the nape of his neck. He was lithe and tanned, and looked like an artist or dancer, a diamond stud twinkling in his left earlobe. Molly had never seen him before. He seemed as excited as Richard, standing close to him, talking animatedly, waving his hands in dramatic flourishes often. Molly noticed his fingers, touching and caressing the blue teapot, its short spout, the pearly-white knob on the teapot cover.

He's probably another of Richard's many collector friends, Molly thought.

Then she saw the same young man, slowly caressing Richard's hands, his five fingers slowly travelling up Richard's right arm, his eyes looking longingly at Richard. Richard did not pull back, instead he returned the young man's intense gaze with a sad and longing smile.

The maker of this is Gan Tjioe Gwat. 'Tjioe' is pronounced 'Chew', written in the old Indo-Dutch spelling. The batik is a combination of tulis and cap, where all the dots are done by hand. Made before World War II, it is from the best quality 'Cap Cent' cotton imported from Europe into Java.

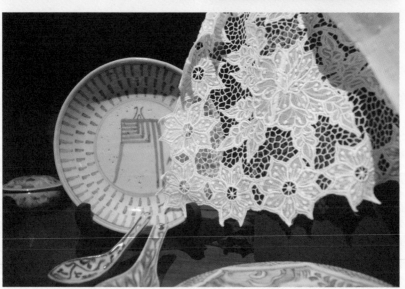

A collection of nyonyaware.

A nyonya kum cheng, *a finger bowl, batik bowl and plates.*

A vintage Pekalongan sarong (top) and a plate with a cricket motif (bottom).

A kebaya and sarong set (top) and an intan, or rose-cut diamond, pendant (bottom).

Ruby and intan *kerosangs and a silver belt.*

Lost in the USA

"HOWDY! HOW Y'ALL DOIN?" yelled the blonde American woman who appeared from nowhere as Liang browsed half-heartedly through the racks for a sweater his size.

"Err ... I'm ... I'm just looking. I'm not doing anything," responded Liang, almost jumping out of his small, thin frame. The woman was dressed smartly in a pencil-slim, tight skirt and a linen shirt with a silk scarf draped stylishly round her neck, her big hair curving upwards on her shoulders sophisticatedly.

"SURE! IF YOU NEED ANYTHING, JUST HOLLER! YOU HEAR ME?" she shouted. Her perfect white teeth gleamed behind glossy rosy-pink lips.

"Err ... must I? Must I holler? Can't I just ask someone nicely?"

"WELL, SIR! IF YOU MUST, THEN YOU MUST! HAVE A VERY GOOD DAY!" she flashed a plastic, sunny smile. It all sounded and looked hollow. She flounced away, her high-heeled shoes clicking down the aisle lined with racks loaded with the latest autumn/winter wear.

It was almost winter and Liang's daughter, Pei Min, had promised him that Texas was one of the best places to live in the US during winter. She was based in Houston working as an auditor in a multinational IT company. She had lived there for years since graduating from an Ivy League college.

Her father knew Pei Min would go places when she started tinkling on the piano at the age of four.

Liang's two sons were also, to his 'misfortune' he jokingly told his friends, too brilliant for the family good for they had left Kuala Lumpur to work overseas in specialised jobs which he hardly understood. His eldest son worked as a genetics research scientist at the Imperial College in London while the other, the creative one who used to spout poetry and rap on the spot, had emigrated to Wellington in New Zealand to work in a renowned computer graphics company, Peter Jackson's gain.

Liang had prayed often to God to bless his family. He prayed that his children would have a good education and reach the pinnacle of success. It had been tough financing their education — he had had to sell off his house and give tuition classes at night after his fulltime job. Perhaps God had been too benevolent or his prayers had been over-zealous, for now, they had all left home finding their homeland devoid of opportunities for their immense talents and capabilities. He didn't mind his sons pursuing career opportunities abroad but had secretly hoped his favourite, his only girl, Pei Min, would return home after her studies overseas.

When she was headhunted for a job in a prestigious organisation immediately after graduating, she had called home to tell her parents in Kuala Lumpur the good news. She could not turn down this offer, she said, and in five years, if she excelled, they would give her the green card.

Liang's heart fell. This was the moment he had dreaded, "But ... but what about us? Both your brothers are already working overseas and now you...? Your mother will be lonely."

"Pa, one phone call. That's all it takes. One call and I'm on my way home if anything happens, you know that. It's a very small world, really. I'll e-mail and skype often, I promise. It's as if I'm right there in the house with you and Ma," Pei Min had assured him.

"But ... but this country needs you, and ... and your mother needs you," he desperately tried to find some reason to make her change her mind.

"Mother is fine with my decision, Pa. She told me to go ahead, break through every glass ceiling nationally and internationally."

"Yeah, that sounds like your mother ... always a rebel ... *heh heh*," he laughed, "But you've always loved this country, the culture, the lifestyle here..."

"You don't have to be in your country to love it, Pa. I will always love my country. But this is an opportunity I cannot turn down. If truth be told, Pa, I'm tired of the racism."

"But ... but ... it's getting better, I promise."

"Give up, Liang," he heard his wife's voice from behind him, "let her go."

Several years later, his wife passed away of illness. Liang's daughter Pei Min grew even closer, calling home from the

US or going on Skype with him every other day. By then, she had two children from a failed marriage.

"Come and visit me, Pa. Travel the world. Come and stay a few months with me, a few months with *Kor Kor* in London, and then with second brother in New Zealand. Three children in three continents. Lucky you, Papa!"

"Yeah, lucky me," he said trying to sound thankful.

He gave all kinds of excuses – the house, the garden, the car, the dog. Now even the dog had died. His latest excuse was he was afraid of the cold.

"No snow, Pa, no snow in Texas except in the mountains. I promise you the weather will be fine. Just lovely clear blue skies and cool weather. An occasional tornado but that's usually in the Midlands. You'll be fine," she'd assured him on the phone.

"Papa, I know you miss her. We all do, but you must move on. She is free now, free of the pain, the drugs, the cancer. You've done everything you can. You mustn't just hole up in the house. Come and stay with me, give it a try first for two months. Then if you like it, stay for as long as you like. Please Pa, I don't want to lose you too," she urged, her voice fraught with worry for her widowed father.

Finally he had relented. There was nothing to hang around for anymore, she was right. A neighbour had promised to take care of the house. Pei Min immediately sent him a ticket, sounding excited on the phone.

"The journey is just twenty-four hours, not that long, Pa. It's not that far. You'll love the USA."

The flight to Houston, Texas, was extremely tiring especially for someone who had never flown anywhere further than Kuala Lumpur to Phuket. He didn't like flying and consented only once to go on a holiday with his wife.

This was his first long haul flight. He found the seats too cramped with inadequate leg room. He felt uncomfortable falling asleep next to the fat, hairy woman snoring beside him; he had never slept beside anyone except his wife.

Going through Immigrations and Customs was even more stressful. When the guards at the Los Angeles international airport asked him to take off his belt, he was outraged. He had never taken off his shoes and belt in public; taking off one's belt felt like undressing, he had argued with the guards in vain. The pockets of air turbulence made him queasy, and he clung to the paper bag for long stretches. He loathed the close proximity to bodies he didn't know, people climbing over him to get to the loo, the body odours, the press and crush and the endless rush.

At dinner that night at his daughter's all-white carpeted home in Memorial Drive, Houston, his daughter asked him about his first visit to the shopping mall.

"So Pa, did you manage to find anything?"

"Yes, I bought a sweater. The saleswoman scared me out of my wits. Why do they talk so loudly here?"

"*Ha ha* ... yeah ... you've got to speak up here or they can't hear you."

"If we yelled like that to my parents, we'd be given two tight slaps for being loud and crass. *Tak seronoh*," he grumbled.

He chewed indifferently at the Shake and Bake chicken his daughter had pulled out of the oven. She had prepared it in a jiffy after coming home late from work. Everything was so nifty here for the homemaker, he observed, full of easy short cuts and bells and whistles.

Clinggg, the oven timer went off indicating the potatoes were ready.

Kachung kachung and a persistent *Beep* and the clothes in the dryer were all nicely spun and dry.

Grrroing, and the heater automatically turned on if the temperature dropped.

Pei Min's two young sons were arguing.

"*Eeewww*, Mom, Shake-and-Bake again? I *wanna* macaroni and cheese!"

"No way! I wanna peanut jelly sandwich ... can I, Mom, *Puhllleease?*"

"*Eeewww*, you can't have sandwich for dinner, silly. Can we have macaroni and cheese in front of the TV, Mom?"

"Yeah, yeah. Like that's so cool, like camping or like ... can we have Coke, Mom?"

"No," snapped Pei Min.

Liang remembered the delicious meals his wife used to cook for him and the children — steaming hot white rice, two to three *lauk* or main dishes, a soup and *sambal* on the side, a curry sometimes. Now her poor grandsons were eating ... gulp ... some gooey American stuff called macaroni and cheese. He missed his rice but dared not utter a squeak. He knew it could not be easy for Pei Min trying to bring up her two boys as a single mother whilst holding a top executive position.

He tried to 'bond' with his grandsons though he couldn't understand their Texan drawl.

"Listen, boys. After dinner, Grandpa will tell you stories, ok? Of the country where I come from, where your mum grew up, the games she played, the antics she and your uncles carried out, your incredible Grandma ... lots of stories to tell."

"*Awww*, must we? *Borinnggg*. We wanna play computer games, Grandpa."

"Another time then," Liang responded, disappointed.

The next morning, Pei Min dropped him off at the Museum of Natural Sciences. He took a stroll through a leafy park and decided to have lunch at the nearby strip-mall. He loathed fast food but without a car to move around, there wasn't much choice. The only restaurants available were one named Soup and Salad and the other was a burger joint. He decided on the burger place because he disliked rich creamy soups and felt like a rabbit on amphetamines when munching on salad. He liked his food hot, temperature-wise as well as taste-wise, and felt miserable eating cold, bland food for lunch.

"FOR HERE OR TO GO, SIR?" the burly African-American woman with short frizzy hair asked loudly.

"Huh ... go where?" he asked puzzled, wondering why the English language had metamorphosed into a different lingo here.

"AH DUNNO. AH DUNNO WHERE YOUSE GOIN. AH AINT GOT NO TIME TO KNOW EFFRYTHAING. FOR HERE OR TO GO?" she shrugged her shoulders, her bosom heaving indignantly.

"Oh just *bungkus* ... err ... I mean, pack it up for me, please ... thank you."

Liang sat on a bench in the afternoon sun looking out on a beautiful lawn. He pulled out his lunch from the styrofoam box and ate the greasy burger slowly, onion specks and tomato sauce dribbling everywhere, the bread was cold and stuck in his throat. He sighed, his thoughts travelled to a faraway place where for a quarter of the price he'd paid, he could get a hot spicy meal with fluffy coconut infused rice, an amazing spicy *sambal*, and thick black coffee from Ipoh or tea from the Cameron Highlands pulled to perfection, a divine frothy mix of flavours.

A man wearing a baseball cap and a Dallas Cowboys teeshirt came and sat next to him, crunching on a packet of corn chips. He looked curiously at the man with the silver wavy hair, who looked a mix of Hispanic, Hawaiian and Chinese struggling with his burger.

"Where're you from, Dude?"

"From Malaysia."

"*Yo!* That's near Thailand, right?"

"Yes, south of Thailand, north of Singapore."

"Hell! I was there back in the seventies! In Nam."

"Oh, you fought in the Vietnam War?"

"Yeah. A long time ago. Came home alive. What you doin' here?"

"Oh just visiting. My daughter works here."

"Man, that's a long way from home, ain't it?"

"Yes. My wife died recently. My daughter persuaded me to visit her here."

"I'm sorry to hear that, I mean, about your wife."

"Yeah, I miss her a lot, think of her all the time. She was special, feisty and stubborn to the very end ... my daughter takes after her, you know."

"Why don't you stay here with your daughter?"

"*Umm* ... I'm seventy-four years old ... it's hard for an old dog to learn new tricks. That's no secret."

"I know. I came back and had to learn new tricks too. Asia ain't like the States."

Pei Min took her father to see what she thought were the entrancing city sights. As they drove past the glittering skyscrapers in downtown Houston, Pei Min tried to persuade her father to reconsider.

"The hospitals here are excellent, the best in the world, the medical care is equal to none. There are laws to protect you, no archaic repressive laws ... you can stand on a soapbox and speak your mind, anytime, anywhere, it's absolute freedom of speech. Yes, there's racism here too, Pa, but if it can be proven in court, the racist goes to jail."

"Really? Wow!" he tried to sound enthusiastic.

He wasn't even sure he could stand on a soapbox for long as his back hurt intermittently and his lips were cracking up from the dry weather. Going trekking with his family into Yosemite or Yellowstone or rafting through the Grand Canyon would be "so cool' as his grandsons would say but he wasn't sure anymore...time was deepening the gap between the will and what the body will do.

"Where do you want to go for lunch, Pa? How about Lobster House or Tex Mex, Pa?"

"Err I miss good ol'*wantan* soup ...can we go to Chinatown?

"But we were just there last weekend at Bellaire."

"Yeah, let's go again."

Pei Min gave her father a good time in the US. She drove him and her children down to San Antonio for the weekend where they rode on the river boats and trams and visited the famous Alamo. She took him to museums, arboretums, flea markets and bookstores in Houston. At night, they would go to the Houston Opera or frequent the theatres. Knowing how much he loved the sea, she drove them to the charming seaside town of Galveston filled with Victorian period architecture and miles of white sandy beaches. They stayed for two nights in a hotel right on the sea front with a spectacular view of the ocean.

Liang loved sitting on the sea wall, enjoying the mighty roar of the Gulf and the tang of the salty spray, watching his grandsons build sandcastles. It brought back memories of the happiest days of his life — his annual holiday with his family to Port Dickson, known as PD, a seaside resort two hours' drive away from Kuala Lumpur.

"This feels just like that sea wall in PD. Remember how you kids would swim and play for hours till you turned brown as *gula melaka*? And remember that mangrove island you used to walk to at low tide? Your Ma was always worried you'd get caught by the tide," Liang reminisced, his eyes lighting up with an aching happiness.

"Yes Pa, I remember those rock pools, strange creatures lurking beneath, and the pink baby crabs racing across the sand banks. How we chased them and yet they outran us! And the *gloop gloop* sounds of the mangrove swamps," Pei Min smiled warmly, her hair tousled by the strong sea breeze.

"I wonder if that chalet is still there. Surrounded by those beautiful casuarinas. I loved sitting on that sea wall, watching the waves crashing on the shore. The sunsets were amazing — golden red sunsets over the Straits of Malacca. Your Ma and I were very happy there ... those were wonderful times."

They were quiet for a while, lost in their own memories as the wind heightened and created little eddies of sand on the beach.

"I want you to throw my ashes there when I die, Pei Min. Cremate me and scatter my ashes there," he said suddenly.

Pei Min's face darkened, "You're not going to die yet, Pa, not for a long time."

"I'm just telling you so you know when the time comes. Be prepared. I was a boy scout, you know," he joked half-heartedly.

A month later, Pei Min was on the Internet trying to book tickets to the Niagara Falls and New York where she planned to take her father.

Liang interrupted her, "Pei Min, please book me a flight home."

"To where?"

"To Kuala Lumpur of course."

"Why so soon? Pa there are many more places I want to show you."

"Haven't you heard of that Ogden Nash saying, something about guests are like fish, they begin to stink after a few days? I have overstayed. It's time to go home."

"You're my father, not a guest! I'm asking you to come and live with me. Grow old here with me, Pa. Give me the privilege of taking care of you."

"I want to return home to Malaysia. I've made up my mind, Pei Min. I want to die in the land of my ancestors. We have been there for more than seven hundred years. I'm an eighth-generation baba. That land runs through my veins, my blood. I am but just a tourist here, but there I am home."

"But there's no one there! Your sons have left. Your grandchildren, your daughter are all here!"

"I have friends, a few ... left," he grimaced.

"I will be fine, Pei Min, don't worry," he tried to assure her, "And remember what you said some time ago about just a phone call away?"

"What's wrong with this country, Pa?"

"Nothing wrong here. It's good, it's been very good. But ... but I don't fit in here. I miss all the familiar things I've grown to love, the sounds, the smells, the colours, the *rojak* of it all. When you're my age, you want to die where your heart is..."

"There you go talking about dying again," she grumbled.

"Metaphorically speaking-*lah*," he grinned.

She saw him off at the George Bush Intercontinental Airport. She knew the answer — he would never return.

When the call for boarding came, she gave him a goodbye hug and whispered, "I envy you, Papa."

"For what?" he asked nonplussed.

"It must be special to have that sense of belonging, that kind of love for one's country."

She kissed him on both cheeks, gave him another bear hug and yelled as she walked away backwards, waving and blowing kisses, "YOU TAKE CARE NOW, Y'ALL HEAR ME? JUST HOLLER IF YOU NEED ME!"

He winced — he never did like the idea of a holler.

My father, Lee Koon Liang, enjoyed travelling but only within this country, being happiest in Port Dickson. He never stepped out of Malaysia.

His last breath on earth was spent helping a friend. He ran over to a neighbour's house early one morning after a distress phone call. His childhood friend, suffering from terminal cancer, had fallen off his bed. After helping his friend back into bed, Papa collapsed and died of a heart attack at the age of 61. At the same moment his friend passed away.

My Papa was much loved for his kindness and helpfulness. It was tragic-heroic he left this way. No goodbyes, just a rush out to help a friend in need and he was gone. A story I have never been able to write.

As a young bridegroom with his bride in 1946.

Photo taken at the same place outside our home in 1978.

The pagi sore (morning-evening) sarong is a clever and practical way of achieving a two-in-one garment. The sarong is divided diagonally into two sections where the motifs are repeated in a different colour. When wrapped from either end, the wearer easily achieves a different look crossing from day to night or vice-versa.

Fakes and copycats were around even in the nineteenth century. The artisanal nature of sarongs was such that batik makers could place their own signatures on their batik creations.

PENANG HOKKIEN IDIOM

Chi lung, Chi pu'ah
Kam cheng ka bay su'ah

One person, one half
Relationship will not be disrupted.

No More Roses

Through the early morning mist, she could make out the outline of a man standing at her mother's grave, a bunch of flowers in his hand. It was a windy morning with a bite in the air, the grassy mounds on the rows of graves glistened with the morning dew. Stately *makaturi* palms in the distance demurred and swayed, ancient angsana trees shading a cluster of graves in a corner rustled mournfully in the wind. She peered through the laden mist at the stranger paying obeisance at her dead mother's resting place. She could not recognise him at all. She stopped and backtracked a few steps, slipping behind a tall thick hedge, speckled with white hibiscus blossoms.

The stranger had not noticed her. He was deep in thought, his head bowed. His shoulders stooped as if he were defeated over a terrible loss. He was tall and distinguished-looking, dressed immaculately in a white dress shirt and dark well-pressed pants. He looked around the same age as her mother if she were still alive, his hair streaked with silver and grey. Gently, he knelt and placed a bouquet of beautiful red roses on her mother's grave.

Roses. Her mother's favourite flowers. Could he be the one? The one who brought the roses last year? Gaik Suan remembered the fading roses lying on her mother's grave when she visited last year after her classes at the university.

They looked forlorn in the late evening, their velvety petals wilting from exposure in the glaring sun. She was puzzled. There were never roses from the family. Her siblings and relatives, she knew, only visited her mother's grave on her mother's death anniversary or during *Qing Ming*, the annual festival to honour the dead, when graves of relatives would be tidied and cleaned, and prayers offered. Only Suan came to visit on her mother's birthday, preferring the peace and privacy compared to the crowds during *Qing Ming*.

"Maybe the roses were from a colleague or an ex-boyfriend," Suan's eldest sister Gaik Bee speculated after Suan told her about the roses the first time.

Her second sister Gaik Lin added, "Mother was a beauty in her younger days according to Grandma. Perhaps they're from a secret admirer. You know ... an unrequited love."

"You're such an incurable romantic, Lin dear," Gaik Bee retorted.

"Maybe they were placed there by mistake," said Suan.

"No way. You can't make mistakes like that, not on clearly marked graves with pricey roses. The roses definitely didn't come from Pa, for sure. He never gave her flowers her entire life. Certainly didn't get them delivered there," commented Gaik Bee caustically, "Was there a note attached, Suan?"

"Nothing. Just twelve red roses," said Suan shaking her head, baffled.

It had rained heavily the night before, a blanket of clouds banked whimsically on the hill slope, shrouding the cemetery. Suan's mother liked it here when she attended her grand aunt's burial years ago on the cool slopes. She asked to be buried at this spot on one of her last few lucid days. The graves were perched on a hill slope facing a lush narrow valley, surrounded by a patchwork of jungle and rubber estates as far as the eye could see.

How did the stranger know where her mother's final resting place would be? She peered from behind the hibiscus hedge — he was still there, kneeling beside the grave, one hand resting gently on the grassy mound where her mother's body lay beneath. Somehow that gesture appeared deeply intimate. Suddenly, he got up as if he could not bear it and strode away swiftly, disappearing behind a row of tombstones, heading in the opposite direction.

Suan was taken aback. She wanted to introduce herself and find out who he was. She ran out from behind the hedge after him and called out, "Wait, wait. Please come back. Come back. Who are you?"

But he was gone, swallowed up in the heavy morning mist.

The whole day at college, she found it difficult to concentrate. Who was he? What was he to her mother? Why had Mother not told her anything about this man? Suan, a second year undergraduate in architecture found the coursework tough and demanding. As the weeks passed, she got more involved in her course assignments and eventually forgot the stranger. Until one day she came across a large chocolate box while cleaning the book shelves in her family home. Suan was busy wiping the fine layer of dust off the shelves where Mother's books still remained, when her hand touched a sturdy box lodged behind a yellowing paperback of *Wuthering Heights*.

It contained her mother's precious mementoes from childhood and school days. Old report cards, school badges, a girl guide book on knots, a black and white photograph of her school choir. Suan scrutinised the photo and spotted her mother — front row, third from the right, the one with the lovely oval-shaped face who was smiling impishly. Other sentimental possessions were a baby book with details of her time of birth, name of doctor and nurse in attendance, inoculations, her first words, first steps, gifts at the first full moon party; a bunch of postcards bound together by a thin orange rubber band, some gold and bronze medals with blue ribbons, an acorn from her first overseas trip to England and a gold pendant in the shape of a key.

Suan was thrilled to find these delightful signposts of her mother's early life — it felt like another way of keeping her close, her memory alive. Mother had died within two months of the shocking prognosis, no time at all to travel to her dream destinations, no opportunity to generate more happy memories. It was a sudden descent into a dark tunnel of disease, racking pain, tubes, injections, syringes, drugs, alcoholic swabs, painkillers and release at the end. After Mother's passing, Suan had kept a simple cotton blouse her mother wore often — a *baju pendek* with two large pockets in front, trimmed with *borderie anglaise* lace. When she ached and yearned for her mother's presence, she would take out her mother's blouse, smell her faint lingering scent, imagine she was still there, vibrantly alive, chatting, laughing, listening to Suan's dreams and problems.

Suan found it hard to get over her grief and loss, although her mother had passed away two years ago at the age of fifty. She had imagined her mother would always be there for as long as it could possibly be, at the milestones of Suan's life, boyfriends, graduation, getting married, having babies, bringing up the children, early adulthood at least and beyond, always there as friend, counsellor, problem-solver. Her life journey ahead felt hollow and lonesome without Mother around.

The last item Suan found in the box was a large brown envelope which looked fairly recent. Puzzled, she pulled out a bunch of cards tied together with a ribbon. Each card had a charming picture of antiquated household things such as a cup and saucer used in the old Chinese coffee shops, a potpourri jar of *bedak sejuk*, a planter's chair, an oil lamp, all evocative of a bygone era.

Unsure of what the cards were for, Suan hesitantly opened the first card and read the message inside scrawled in a slanted handwriting,

> *I know it can never be. You have told me clearly it is impossible, and that you cannot leave him till your youngest has reached twenty-one years of age. I respect that. I know I have no claim, no claim at all except that I love you. I have loved you, loved you from the moment I first saw you. I will wait. I will wait for you even if it takes forever. You are worth waiting for, even if it's a lifetime.*

Suan dropped the card, reeling in shock. She was the youngest in the family, she had turned twenty-one two years ago. Was the phrase 'your youngest' referring to her? Was her existence some kind of hindrance to something bigger, of far greater meaning than her? Suan had celebrated her twenty-first birthday at home with family and friends, she remembered her mother seemed agitated that night, even distraught. Mother excused herself before the party ended, quite unlike her and went to bed early. When Suan went to check on her, she found her mother crying in bed.

"What's the matter, Mama?"

"Nothing."

"Something's wrong. Why are you crying?"

"It's nothing. I'm happy for you, that's all. You're twenty-one years old, an adult now."

"Oh Ma, please, are you alright? I'll get you a glass of warm water. Maybe you're coming down with something."

"No, I'm fine. Suan, forgive me."

"For what?"

"Forgive me if I should leave one day."

Suan remembered touching her mother's forehead, wondering if she were delirious. It felt cold and clammy but Mother insisted she was alright and pushed her out of the room, urging her to return to her birthday celebrations.

Fits of anxiety and bewilderment knotted themselves tighter and tighter in her stomach. The stranger kneeling at her mother's grave, the red roses last year and this year, and now this note, this bundle of cards.

Trembling, not knowing what to expect next, Suan picked up another card. Again there were no names, no dates, just a few lines which raged with despair and anger in the same handwriting.

> *I wish I'd never met you. I curse the day I did. Get out, get out of my head, go away. You have no right, no right to be in my mind, my brain. I have no right to hold you in my heart ... I want to forget you if that is possible. I have met other women, beautiful intelligent women, but ... but nothing compares to you ... nothing. I'm trying to forget you and move on. I am working hard on this, working hard to try and forget you but it is impossible. I find myself thinking of you all the time, in all spaces, in all places.*

Riveted, compelled to follow this discordant symphony, Suan selected yet another card with a picture of a *tengkak*, an enamel tiffin carrier in blue and white. Inside the card lay a poem,

> *The smell of rain hits me*
> *Like staccato beating canvass*
> *To sag under the sky's insistence*
> *I think of you*
>
> *The sound of coffee as I simmer*
> *My thoughts delicious and dark*
> *Inside my mind grim persistence*
> *I think of you*
>
> *The images of you as I breathe*
> *In ever-shifting circles and squares*
> *My aching heart zero resistance*
> *I think of you*

Suan felt her heart pounding faster than normal. She tried to remember desperately the sequence of events. When her mother was diagnosed with cancer three months after Suan's twenty-first birthday, Mother called the family together and told them the terrible news.

Suan was appalled and asked her mother, "Why?"

"Why what?" responded her mother, puzzled.

"Why didn't you tell me? You knew all along, didn't you?"

"No, Suan. I didn't know. I only learnt about this today from the doctor," Mother replied looking surprised.

"Then why did you say you would leave? You said that on my twenty-first birthday, remember? Upstairs in your room?" questioned Suan, distressed at the terrible news.

Suan's mother kept silent for a while, her face inscrutable. She looked out of the window to a distant invisible place. Then she turned to Suan and said wryly, "It doesn't matter. Looks like I will have to leave after all, sometime soon. In one way or another."

"How soon is soon?" asked her daughters.

"The doctor told me I have six more months to live. Or six more months to die, depending on how you want to look at it," she said trying to smile. Her calm, taut voice could not hide the devastation on her face.

Suan covered her face with her hands as jumbled thoughts whirled crazily in her head. She splayed her fingers apart and watched the tiny particles of dust floating in lazy spirals in the shafts of sunlight streaming in through the windows.

Did she love him too the way he loved her? Or was this a one-sided love affair? Was she crazy to think of leaving and losing everything? And if she didn't care about father, what about us, her daughters? Was that why she stayed on? If she had gone to him, would she still be alive today? Perhaps ...

perhaps this love might have brought her happiness, sustain her, even save her.

Eldest sister often dropped hints that if she were Mother, she would have walked out of the marriage a long time ago. It was 'as dead as a door nail', according to Gaik Bee. Their parents were cordial to each other although Father was seldom around, involved in his expanding business empire. Mother had everything she could possibly need but seemed restless and lonely.

Once she commented to her daughters when she took them shopping, "Your father asked me to use my supplementary credit card to buy something for my birthday. Anything at all, no limits. He can't find the time, so he says."

Gaik Bee suggested, "How about a diamond necklace from Tiffany's? That would jolt him to his senses."

"Good idea," she laughed half-heartedly then said spontaneously, "What I really want is something that cannot be bought."

"What can't money buy, Ma?" Gaik Lin wanted to know.

"What do you want, Ma?" asked Suan.

"Love," her mother answered softly.

Dust, dust everywhere, Suan noticed, on the shelves, the floor, the windows, she really must get the room cleaned properly. Some dust is best left untouched, Suan reflected. No one would know of these love letters except her, not even her sisters, certainly not her father. She tore the cards into pieces, took the shredded bits downstairs to the garden and burnt them.

Suan continued visiting her mother's grave every year on her mother's birthday, and every year, without fail, she would find twelve red roses on the grave, their brooding, dark-red mesmerising, foreboding, their petals soft and luxurious to the touch. She would pick up a rose and sniff its scent — luscious and sweet, with hints of a beautiful secret garden, transient, unattainable. She never bumped into the stranger again.

Then, it happened.

One day, ten years later, Suan, now an architect, found there were no more roses. The grave looked lonesome and bare without the blazing-red, lustrous blooms. The stranger disappeared as mysteriously as he had appeared in the first encounter years ago. Perhaps he had found someone else or maybe, he too had passed away. She would never know what really happened. It would remain a secret as foggy as that dew-drenched morning when she encountered an undying love of a man for a woman who lay buried beneath.

Bouquets of roses feature in this work by Van Zuylen, famous for introducing the buketan style (floral bouquet) and the use of pastel colours. Eliza C. Van Zuylen started a workshop in Pekalongan in the late nineteenth century and by 1918, owned one of the biggest batik workshops run by an Indo-European in Java.

Roses on the kepala (head) of the sarong. This Dutch-influenced piece originates from Pekalongan in 1938 at the Van Zuylen workshop. (Courtesy of Hartono's Collection)

About the Author

Lee Su Kim is a Malaysian writer whose creative, literary and cultural activist endeavours and scholarly works have received considerable attention in Southeast Asia and internationally.

Her light touches of humour, dry wit, sharp observations and fluid prose can be enjoyed in her three bestsellers *Malaysian Flavours: Insights into Things Malaysian, Manglish: Malaysian English at its Wackiest* and *A Nyonya In Texas: Insights of a Straits Chinese Woman in the Lone Star State.*

Her first collection of short stories, *Kebaya Tales: Of Matriarchs, Maidens, Mistresses and Matchmakers* is another bestseller. In 2013, it was awarded the national Popular-Star Readers Choice Awards.

She was born in Kuala Lumpur to a baba from Malacca and a nyonya from Penang. Educated in the Bukit Bintang Girls' School, Kuala Lumpur, Su Kim holds a Bachelor of Arts in English, a Diploma and Masters in Education from the University of Malaya, Kuala Lumpur. She lived in the US for four years and earned a Doctorate in Education from the University of Houston in 2001.

Formerly Associate Professor at the School of Language Studies & Linguistics, Universiti Kebangsaan Malaysia where she lectured and researched on language, culture and identity, she is now a fulltime writer, language trainer and consultant.

She is the founding President of the Peranakan Baba Nyonya Association of Kuala Lumpur & Selangor, formed in 2008. She enjoys and shares cultural complexity beyond cuisine, *sarong kebaya* and *kasut manik* as a frequent presenter of the rich diversity of being nyonya. Her website is at www.leesukim.net

Also by the author:
- *Malaysian Flavours: Insights into Things Malaysian (1st and 2nd editions)*
- *Manglish: Malaysian English at its Wackiest*
- *A Nyonya In Texas: Insights of a Straits Chinese Woman in the Lone Star State*
- *Kebaya Tales: Of Matriarchs, Maidens, Mistresses and Matchmakers*